EMERGE

THE EDGE

~~~

Book 1.5

A Prequel Novella

PRAISE FOR THE EMERGE SERIES
2015 International Book Awards Finalist

Originality is the distinguishing characteristic of this story! Young Adult Fantasy has been pumped out like never before, but Melissa A. Craven has skillfully developed an Urban Fantasy set in a real life, believable context. I can almost believe this ancient race of Immortals actually lives among us.
~ Hub Pages Reviewer

Emerge – The Awakening grabbed my attention within the first few pages and refused to let go until the very end.
~ Jamie Georgianson for Readers' Favorite

Never once when reading did I stop and think, this kind of reminds me of (whichever book insert here). Bottom line, get this book. It's amazing and worthy of your time. Warning though... you might get obsessed.
~ The Book Goddess

This was such an impressive start to a unique new series. The characters are the true stars, they grew with the story and were portrayed realistically with their stroppy attitudes, tantrums and snark. Allie was a breath of fresh air when it came to heroines. She was totally badass.
~ Literary-ly Obsessed

Emerge: The Awakening is a story that begins as a single snowflake and ends in an avalanche. Melissa A. Craven has put together a story that unfolds and unfolds and unfolds again, revealing characters of unusual depth.
~ Amazon Reviewer

From the first page to the last, Melissa A. Craven has a talent for keeping her reader's attention as she reveals Allie's story, layer by interesting layer. And when you get to the last page, you are left wanting more!
~ Amazon Reviewer

EMERGE

THE EDGE

MELISSA A. CRAVEN

Midnight Hour Studio
Atlanta

EMERGE: The Edge Copyright © September 29, 2015

By: Melissa A. Craven

Midnight Hour Studio INC

Atlanta, Georgia

This book is a work of fiction. Names, characters, businesses, organizations, places, events and incidents either are the product of the author's imagination or are used fictitiously. Any resemblance to actual persons, living or dead, events, or locales is entirely coincidental.

For more information contact: info@midnighthourstudio.com or visit the author's website at www.melissaacraven.com

Book cover design by: Zoe Shtorm

Interior design by: Melissa A. Craven

Melissa@thewriterlab.com

ISBN-13: 978-0-9909819-2-3

ISBN-10: 0-9909819-2-4

First Midnight Hour Studio Print Edition: September 29, 2015

DEDICATION

This one is for Mom
Because she always liked the long version best.

ACKNOWLEDGMENTS

Words cannot express how grateful I am to my family. The last six months since Emerge: The Awakening was launched has been an incredible roller coaster ride for us all. I could not have done any of this without the love and support of you all. To my sister, Angela and my mother, Debby, who is the only one who will still talk to me about my book without rolling her eyes. This book is for you, Mom! And to my awesome dad, David, for giving me his very special gift of sarcasm.

To the one who shall remain nameless, thank you for your countless hours of acting as my sounding board and dealing with my narcissism and one-track mind. I literally could not have done this without you. And to everyone I ever asked to read the loong version—I'm so sorry, it was terrible! But The Edge is the result of all those tireless long drafts. I hope you all enjoy it! To Jenny, I love you but, seriously, get out of my brain! To my uncles, Kerry and Chris, thank you both so much for your valuable input. Stacey Randolph, Kayla Howarth and Michelle Lynn, your feedback was incredible! To all my other beta readers, thank you so much for your enthusiasm.

To my editors, Amber J Chapman and Deb Bedell, thank you for all your help! And to Zoe Shtorm for the amazing cover art, yet again! And thank you also, to YABooksCentral.com for hosting the cover reveal and book launch!

A big thank you to the city of Cleveland for all the wonderful memories and providing the perfect setting for Emerge. And to Kelleys Island especially. The island as it is portrayed in the book is purely fictional, but is based on the real Kelleys Island near Sandusky, Ohio. Finally, I thank God for the constant reminder that I am doing what I am supposed to be doing. Over the years, circumstances always bring me back to writing—my favorite thing to do in the whole world.

ONE

"I can't believe I'm back here again." Aidan glared up at the Art Deco gates of Cliffton Academy like they were the bars to his prison cell. The school was a small, but elite community that provided Aidan and his friends with some semblance of a normal life. He just wasn't sure if he could face another year of pretending to be someone he wasn't.

I'm going to suffocate here. It took everything he had to cross the perfectly manicured lawns teeming with students and teachers. Fountains splashed and shimmered. Winding paths and small, gated alcoves branched off from the courtyard here and there, offering intimate shaded corners of respite from the late July heat. The gardens were bursting with colorful flowers and the Lake Erie breeze drove the noise of the bustling city center into the distance. It was all such a pleasant picture, but Aidan wanted to run in the opposite direction.

Time to suck it up and do this. He sighed, but the deep ache in his chest reminded him he was still healing.

"Can't be that bad already?" Quinn slapped his back, making Aidan draw in a sharp breath.

"Sorry, I forgot! Still sore?"

"It's alright. I'm just so exhausted, and coming back to this place isn't exactly conducive to my recovery."

"I know. It sets my teeth on edge to be back here again. I don't know, man, maybe you should've stayed in Tibet a few more weeks. You aren't back to your normal self yet." Quinn gave him a worried look.

"I'll take school any day over that place."

"Take it easy today, Aidan. Try not to let it all get to you."

"Yeah, sure." Aidan shrugged, wincing at the tug of torn muscle not quite healed.

"Quinn!" Sasha waved him over to a group of her friends.

"Looks like I've been paged."

"Go. I'm fine." Aidan slid his earbuds into place, selecting Elgar's *Serenade in E-minor* for a soothing distraction. He gazed around the quad at all the eager faces and groups of friends reuniting after six weeks of vacation. And then he noticed the wide arch of empty space surrounding him and the way everyone waved and called out to him, but never ventured close. Aidan's reality came slamming back into him like a punch in the gut.

Here we go again. He'd spent the last six weeks with his kind. Now he was back in the mortal world where everything that sucked about being Aidan was ten times worse. Their extreme reactions to his power sucked, but he was used to that. It was the onslaught of all their mortal pain that was difficult for him to manage. Every knee scrape, paper cut, and broken bone—every hurt feeling, bruised ego, and heart-wrenching breakup, Aidan faced it with them.

Immortals processed pain in a very different way. It still hurt like hell, but it was fleeting. With mortals, the pain lingered longer and was more poignant. Coming back after so many weeks away, it would be difficult to get used to it again. He was just beginning to learn how to erect a barrier between himself and everything they felt, but it required an incredible amount of concentration and a level of focus he'd completely neglected over the past two months.

They just feel too damn much!

At that moment, everyone around him was happy and in high spirits, which he didn't get to experience with them. As a healer, Aidan only got the sorrow, never the joy.

"Hey Aidan!" Jason called across the quad. Aidan waved back, feeling his spirits lift at the sight of a familiar face. Jason was a teammate and a long time friend. He wasn't too complicated or bright, but he was loyal. There were a few other friendly faces around, like Kayla and the rest of the football team. People who would be happy to see him.

Definitely better than Tibet.

If Aidan could have a do-over, he would've made drastically different decisions that night, almost two months ago. It was just before the end of the school term and he was bored and more than ready for the escape of summer vacation. There was a party, he'd been drinking from Gregg's special stash—the kind that was slightly more potent to Immortals and therefore off limits. The small flask was just enough to make Aidan feel a little reckless, and a lot stupid. Racing the train seemed like a fun idea at the time; the thrill of driving fast, speeding along the tracks until he pulled ahead of the engine. But it was the turn that threw everything off. He should've been able to make it in plenty of time, but he took it too fast and lost control of the car. She didn't make it. Even now, his heart lurched at the memory of his beautiful, but completely totaled Maserati. He'd missed the train, but rolled his car down a hill and wrapped it around a tree.

What was I thinking? But it was just another one of those reckless moments when Aidan was so desperate for a distraction he acted impulsively. The mess that followed was a total nightmare and the look of disappointment on his father's face still haunted him.

Aidan vividly remembered the moment of impact; the screech of the train trying to stop, the blare of the whistle as it sailed past, narrowly missing him. The crunch of metal. The way his body bounced around as the car tumbled. The excruciating pain as he slammed into the tree, the sound of glass shattering and then silence, as the closest thing to death he might ever know, took him. He was out for nearly three weeks while his body regenerated. When he woke, he was in a clinic in the mountains of Tibet and the worst of it was over, but it would still take many more months before he was completely recovered.

Aidan's journey to Tibet was a long road of lies and deception that led to tampering with medical records, coroner's reports, and a lot of memories. When Aidan was pulled from the wreckage, he was dead; every bone in his body, broken. He was packed off to the morgue where his brothers had to break in to steal his body. They shipped him to Bangladesh in a coffin, and Jin traveled with him to the remote mountains of the Himalayas. Aidan spent the entire summer there as he slowly healed from all the visible wounds. The pain of regeneration was tolerable, but he'd never felt so weak and disconnected from his power. And here he was, months later, and he still felt lost and alienated from the person he was before he "died."

There was a Senate hospital in Lisbon, Portugal, where young Immortals could go while they recovered from grievous injuries, but Aidan's healing gift made it impossible for him to be around other patients. Instead, Gregg sent him to Abbot Jing Zong and the Monastery where Aidan was the only Immortal in residence. He nearly lost his mind from the boredom.

Aidan worried that he would have to face criminal charges for his reckless behavior. He'd risked discovery and caused far too much effort to cover up his death. His behavior did not reflect well on Naeemah and Gregg in their position as Governor, but somehow, it all went away while he was recovering. The Senate left it to his parents to discipline him, which hadn't really worked out in his favor. He wouldn't be driving again until after graduation—in two years. And his allowance was going directly into his college fund for the next year.

"How was your summer, Aidan?" He snapped out of his reverie to find a pretty brunette staring up at him expectantly.

Crap, what was her name? He tugged on his headphones. She was his lab partner just last term.

"Short." His tone was unintentionally harsh and Aidan watched in dismay as she stammered and rushed away.

Then he remembered.

I am such an asshole. He watched her retreating figure, wanting to run after her but he knew that would only make it worse. Her name was Eva and she was mildly Autistic. It was a secret she kept locked up so tightly, she often made herself, and Aidan, sick over it. She was highly functional, but her limitations were mostly social.

He remembered how difficult it was for her to work so closely with him in chem lab last term. For the first few weeks, she went entirely mute whenever he spoke directly to her. By the end of their last semester together, Aidan had coaxed her out of her shell and they'd become hesitant friends. And he'd just scared her to death on a day that was already a huge challenge for her.

Aidan slid his earbuds back in place and made his way toward the symphony hall. Mortal girls always had such strong reactions to him. Sometimes they were flustered and frightened, much like Eva. Other girls reacted to him obsessively, following him around campus like an annoying, giggling, whispering shadow. In middle school he discovered that flirting shamelessly sent them scurrying away.

Guys were different. They were either mildly okay with him as long as he didn't get too close or it went to the other extreme, and they absolutely despised him for no other reason than his power made them uneasy.

His Immortal family also responded to his powerful nature, but they tried to hide it for his sake. Some were better at it than others, but it still stung when even his own mother balked at his touch. At sixteen, Aidan was already the most powerfully gifted Immortal of his generation. Probably the most powerful in many generations. His friends always deferred to him, which he ignored most of the time, but it was a lonely life when everyone's natural inclination was to keep him respectfully at arms length.

He knew his family loved him and it hurt them to see how much he suffered in his isolation, so he did what he could to put their fears to rest. He pretended. Aidan was the epitome of the jovial, cocky, all American high school boy everyone expected him to be. He smiled and cracked jokes. He flirted with the cheerleaders and he played football. He went to crazed parties and routinely got into trouble. He was the guy everyone wanted around, but no one wanted to approach. He was a total fake. But with mortals, it worked. It made him something they could understand. With his family, his pretense erased their looks of pity and concern. But he'd done it for so long, he wasn't sure who he was anymore.

"Aidan, walk me to class?" He turned to see a beautiful blond marching toward him with determination.

Headphones are the universal sign for leave me alone. How is this difficult? He reluctantly tugged on his earbuds again.

"Hey, sweetheart." He put his mask firmly in place as he flirted with the vapid girl.

"Sucks coming back, doesn't it? I heard you spent the summer in Spain. We were in Madrid. You should have called."

"I was in Bangladesh, actually," he lied.

"That's Spain, right?" Her brow puckered in confusion.

"No. No it isn't." *Check out Google maps, babe. Just once in a while, give it a little spin.*

"Aidan! Got a minute?" Graham waved him over.

"Sorry, sweetheart. Gotta run." Aidan left her blinking in confusion to join Graham by the steps of the Symphony Hall.

"Dude, you looked like you were drowning there. You sure you're doing alright?" Graham asked. "Maybe you should take another week or two off."

"I just need to get back to normal. If I'm forced to rest any more, I'll lose my freaking mind."

"Is it extra weird this time?" Graham asked. "Coming back after so much time away from all this lying and hiding?"

"You're on the cusp, man. A few more weeks and you're the newbie." Aidan gave him a playful shove.

"Happy birthday to me."

"It's normal," Aidan said.

"What?"

"Feeling scared shitless."

"I kinda wish I didn't know it was coming. I feel like a ticking time bomb."

"I wish I could say the wait is worse than the Awakening," Aidan said.

"Thanks. You're a big help." Graham rolled his eyes. "See ya later."

"Later." Aidan took the steps up to the symphony hall two at a time. It was his favorite place on campus—on just about any other day. Today it was a reminder that he could be heading toward a very different symphony hall. If he was a normal guy. He'd received the offer from the Musical Conservatory of Vienna, Austria last year. Of course he couldn't go. Vienna was the last place any Immortal would step foot willingly. It was the headquarters of the Coalition. He'd be a fool to even consider accepting their offer. But God, he wanted it. It was the opportunity of a lifetime and it killed him to turn it down.

Other schools were interested. He had a standing offer with the Cologne University of Music in Germany, but his parents wouldn't let him leave until he had a few years of training under his belt. Just six months after his Awakening was the wrong time. Logically, he knew that. But it didn't change his desperate need to use music as an escape.

Stepping into the orchestra pit lifted his spirits more than anything else could have. His position as first violinist and Concertmaster of the Cliffton Orchestra was the best thing about school. That and football were the closest he ever got to normal life.

"Hey Aidan!"

He nodded toward the group of giggling flutists as he made his way to his seat. The familiar scent of horsehair and the piney aroma of freshly applied rosin snapped him out of his irritable mood as he checked out the sheet music for the day. They would be doing scales and warm-ups for the first hour. Too many students who hadn't picked up their instruments all summer would need the practice.

"Great." Scales drove him batshit.

"At least we're running through Tchaikovsky's *Concerto in D-Major* in the second hour," a familiar voice said. "But we'll be lucky if we get through the first movement."

"Wendy!" He was surprised by how happy he was to see her. She was first cellist and one of the most musically gifted mortals he'd ever performed with.

"I have a bone to pick with you, McBrien!" She glared at him.

"What'd I do?" He bit back his laughter. She was trying so hard to tell him off, but the result was more comical than scary.

"Racing trains? Are you a complete moron?" She swatted him with her bow. "Your stupid antics got you suspended and I had to learn *Tambourin Chinois* two *days* before the final show of the year!"

That was the official story. As far as the school knew, Aidan's race against the train ended in his favor, but the police didn't think it was very funny. The school didn't either when the story landed in the papers a few days later. Cliffton had a zero tolerance policy for such behavior, so he was suspended for the last two weeks of the term for "publicly dishonoring the school."

"Come on, Wen, you know Kreisler better than I do!"

"Yo Yo Ma's arrangement is difficult! And there were members of the Cleveland Orchestra in attendance! I nearly lost my mind preparing for two solos! Don't you ever do that to me again! Not to mention you could have been killed and I wouldn't have anyone to practice with this year!"

"I missed you too." They'd been friends for years, but it always felt more like a professional relationship centered on their love of music. Wendy was less affected by Aidan than most girls and he thought it had something to do with the fact that she wasn't attracted to him at all. He, along with every other male in school, wasn't her type, but she still liked to keep her distance. Wendy's girlfriend, Anya, however, *loathed* him and was jealous of the time they spent practicing.

"Missed hearing you play this summer, Aidan." The cute viola player blushed furiously as she took her seat behind the conductor's stand.

"Yeah, we missed you at the final symphony," another violinist added.

"Sorry about that, sweetheart." He slipped back into his role. Somehow he'd eased out of it with Wendy.

He watched Wendy take her place just opposite him and felt a genuine smile light his face. She was seriously hot, with long dark hair lit with auburn highlights and big hazel eyes she happened to be rolling at him.

"Oh no, don't turn those big brown eyes on me!"

"What?"

"I'm not part of your weird little fan club, McBrien." She waved her bow at him.

"Thank God for that," he said dryly.

"So when are we practicing?" She busied herself with applying fresh rosin to her bow.

"After lunch?"

"'K, come find me here."

"Hi Aidan! Have a nice summer?" The greetings continued to echo all around him.

"Yeah, thanks, sweetheart." He rolled his eyes at Wendy.

"They do seem to buzz around you like flies on sh—"

"Hey!"

"Su-gar," she amended with a chuckle.

"I think all the flirty is worse than last year."

"I suppose you do have that tall, dark and dangerous

thing going for you. Especially after that BS stunt with the train. And the rippling tattooed muscles probably don't hurt either."

"I do have other qualities." Aidan felt his face flush at her blatant scrutiny.

"Aw, you're blushing! Athletic, Mr. Football with a trust fund, genius IQ, and a violin prodigy well on your way to becoming a virtuoso at sixteen! Plagued by every hot girl in the school. You poor thing!"

"You're not so bad yourself. Too bad I'm not a girl." He winked.

"Well, you can't have everything. It wouldn't be fair."

※※※

"Cheer up, little brother. High school won't last forever," Sasha said.

"I know." He leaned against the railing beside her on the ferry deck. After the full school day, they still had an afternoon of endless training ahead of them, but Aidan was already exhausted. "I know going back is always an adjustment, but now that we're manifested, it was a lot harder, wasn't it?"

"A million times harder." She gazed across the water and he could tell the struggle to get through the day had taken its toll on her as well.

"Sometimes I wish I could just get my GED and move on," he said.

"Right, Dad would have a coronary. You know how he is about education."

"Yeah, yeah, yeah, no formal education until the sixteenth century, before that he was an uneducated soldier with limited means," Aidan said in a bored tone. "It's just in another life Vienna would've happened this year."

"I'm sorry, Aidan. But it's not your only offer. What about Germany?"

"I have to graduate first. I know the Cologne University of Music is just as good, but it's two years away."

"Don't take this the wrong way, but I'm glad you're not going yet. It's too damn far. I'm not ready."

"I know. How will I ever get by without you there to irritate me?" He smiled in a way he only did for Sasha. She was irritating as hell, but they were as close as two adopted siblings could be.

"You'll be so busy, you'll hardly notice I'm not there with you," Sasha said.

"That's highly unlikely. It will be far too quiet."

"Don't ever do that to me again," she whispered. "Two months without even a phone call."

"I'm sorry, sis."

"It was a lousy summer." Sasha leaned her head on his shoulder.

"I'm sorry about Quinn." Things had fallen apart for them again while he was gone.

"For some reason, it just never seems to work for us. We're just better as friends."

"I really missed you, Sash."

"Listen, I know it's harder for you than the rest of us, but maybe this year will be different?" She nudged him playfully.

"Maybe it will." He draped his arm across her shoulders, ignoring the ripple of tension she didn't often show.

TWO

"You from Wellington?" The question caught Allie off guard. Most people just ignored her. Even now, as she stood on the crowded ferryboat, there was a visible radius of emptiness around her.

Allie glanced helplessly after her dad's retreating figure. Carson had gone to find food since they still had several hours before they would reach the docks at Wellington Harbor on North Island. Carson was her buffer. He always diffused these horrifyingly awkward situations.

"Yeah, we moved there almost two years ago." Allie stared over the boy's shoulder at the icy blue waters of Cook Straight. Avoiding eye contact was a nervous habit she'd adopted over the past few years. She didn't do well with people—boys especially. These things always started with an initial harmless interaction. Just like now with his response to her unique features; the vibrant red hair that shimmered like fire in the sun, her intense but weird green eyes that were slightly tilted, giving her a hint of the exotic, the smattering of freckles, the voluptuous figure, blah, blah, blah. Then came his flustered reaction when he took a step too close. Some nervous chatter would follow as he grew increasingly uncomfortable and then he'd look for a quick escape or make up some excuse to be anywhere else.

"Where do you go to school?" He leaned against the railing beside her. She saw the way he hesitated, like he'd already changed his mind about approaching her. But this boy was more intrigued with her than most. He was intimidated, but fascinated at the same time. The realization came to her as clearly as a thought and it left her unsettled. For as much time as she spent alone, Allie was a good judge of character. Probably a result of a life of observation without much participation. But there were times when her unusually strong intuition actually scared her.

"St. Catherine's." Allie shifted her gaze down to her boots. Another nervous habit.

"Hey, I go to St. Patrick's!"

And this is exactly why I go to the all girls' school.

"I'm Ethan." He reached to shake her hand.

Oh, you don't want to do that, Ethan.

"I'm Allie." She took his hand with a timid smile, but her smiles never worked. As soon as his trembling fingertips grasped hers, he pulled away like she'd branded him with her touch.

"Nice meeting you." He shoved his hands back into his coat pockets as he inched away.

"You too." She cast her eyes back down to her shuffling feet. Forging new friendships just never worked out for her, and somewhere along the way, she stopped trying. Most of the time she was happiest when left to her own devices.

"Maybe I'll see you around after school sometime. St. Pat's is just across the park." Ethan's tone was polite, but she knew he just wanted to bail.

"Yeah, sure." Allie nodded.

"I-uh, have to get back to my friends. We're uh-docking soon, you know." And with that, Ethan turned and fled.

"Have a nice afternoon." She watched his quick retreat. They were adrift in the Tasman Sea, somewhere between North and South Island of New Zealand. They wouldn't dock for hours yet.

∽∾∽

"I've got pizza!" Carson called across the deck. "Let's get out of this cold wind!"

"Great! I'm starving," Allie said.

"Nice try, kid. You okay? I saw you with that boy."

"I'm fine, Dad." Allie sighed as they ducked into the heated lounge room to grab one of the last empty tables. "Better now." She took a huge bite of gooey, cheesy pizza. She felt like she should be more upset by these things, but now that it was over, she was just relieved.

"It won't always be like that."

"I know."

"There's not a thing wrong with you, honey."

"I'm weird, Dad. I just don't know how to talk to people."

"Weird's not a bad thing. And give the guy some credit. When I was his age, I tripped over my own tongue when I first met your mother. Couldn't string a coherent sentence together, but I eventually found my voice and look at us now."

"Boring old married couple?"

"Boring? I still learn something new about your mom everyday."

"You two are perfect together."

"You'll find that too someday."

"I'd be happy with just a few friends, Dad. I'm only fifteen."

"Same age I was when I met your mom."

"People don't marry their high school sweethearts anymore."

"Well, we spent years and years apart when college led us in different directions. It was incredible luck that we found each other again, but the time apart was essential for us. We got to figure out who we were as individuals before we reconnected and picked up right where we left off. I've never stopped thanking my old college professor for bringing us together again to teach at the same university."

"Well, I'm lucky you two happened to be in South Africa at just the right time to adopt me. The way you guys hop around the globe, it's a friggin' miracle you ever found me."

"And a fortunate day that was for all of us. Your sister took one look at you and refused to put you down. We had to take you home after that. You were nothing but crazy red hair and big green eyes."

"Thanks, Dad." Allie smiled.

"For what?"

"Making me feel better."

"I was an awkward kid, Allie. Trust me, it will get

better. I know it's harder because we move so much, but I would love to see you try. You've given up and that kills me."

"I like my alone time. I mean, it would be nice to have some friends to hang out with occasionally, but I'm okay by myself. I like my own company and I think I do a pretty good job of keeping myself entertained."

"You're an introvert, like me. You don't rely on other people for your happiness. But that doesn't mean you don't need people."

"I know. I just need to find the right kind of people, I guess."

"You think she'll remember we're coming home today?" Carson asked, steering them away from the sensitive subject.

"Who, Mom? No way. She'll be sitting at her messy desk covered in old teabags with no food in the house."

"And having the time of her life working on her research without interruption." He and Allie had spent the last week on a ski trip to Aoraki Mount Cook on South Island, while Allie was on holiday from school.

"You think she finished?" Allie asked. Lily stayed behind at their home along the Rona bay on North Island to work on her latest research project with her grad students from Victoria University. Something about cataloguing the events that shaped prehistoric New Zealand. Lily found the project exciting, but Allie's eyes tended to glaze over whenever her mom talked about her work.

"Probably not."

Allie breathed a sigh of relief. That project was the thing that kept them in New Zealand. When Lily finished, they would likely move again. She knew she could handle the change. She always did. It was just so much easier to stay where they were. But it would be Carson's turn to take the next assignment. And Allie, like her sister Joscelin before her, would tag along for the ride.

Allie felt it coming—another big change. She wouldn't be surprised this time.

⚉⚉⚉

"Almost home!" Carson drove past the Days Bay ferry at the Eastbourne docks. "I've enjoyed our trip, but I missed your mom."

"Me too." The weeklong ski trip was nice. Allie always enjoyed these trips with her dad. She just wasn't sure it was enough anymore. Lately, she spent a lot of time watching other kids her age, longing to participate. She just didn't know how to breach the gap between her and the rest of the world.

"We'll probably have to go out for dinner if we want to eat actual food." Carson drove through their neighborhood to their shabby little beach bungalow on the corner. It was white and yellow with an acid green door and of all the places they'd lived, it felt the most like home.

Carson reached for his phone as he made the final turn to park on the street.

"Who's that?" Allie felt a strange shiver setting her hair on end. She recognized the young woman standing on their front porch, but Allie knew she'd never seen her before. The woman moved quickly down the steps, retreating to her car. She was so angry, afraid and confused all at once. Allie had sensed such things before, but this time it was intense. Like she could actually feel the woman's frustrations.

"Dad, who is that?" She was tall, with her dark hair pulled severely back from her beautiful face. There was something familiar about the way she moved, graceful and fluid, like she was comfortable with her height and slender limbs. Halfway to her car, she turned to stare at Allie in surprise.

How can I know someone I've never met?

"That's just one of Lil's grad students," Carson said as he turned the car around. "I think we've seen her at the house before."

Her father was lying. Allie would have remembered this woman.

"Your mother wants us to pick up dinner." He headed toward the neighborhood market.

Allie turned to stare at the woman standing in the middle of the street. She met her cold, gray eyes and felt a stab of fear tingle along her spine.

She came here searching for something and didn't find the answers. Allie felt an overwhelming desire to connect with her, but something about this woman was dangerous.

"Come on, Allie." Carson hopped out of the car at the market. "Mom wants fresh salmon."

"Coming, Dad." Allie swallowed the questions rising in her throat. Carson didn't want her to meet that woman, and she knew better than to ask why.

THREE

"Parry!" Greggory McBrien commanded as Aidan countered his advance. "Botta dritta." He spoke the forms in Italian, wanting to see a straightforward attack and thrust. Aidan complied, but he hated this technical aspect of his training.

"Again! And do not lead with your dagger," Gregg drawled in his soft Scottish brogue. "Your dagger is always—"

"I know, I know! It's a second line of defense, never the first." Aidan returned to guard, checking his stance before he attempted a *seconda*, a swift cut and thrust with his rapier blade at a precise forty-five degree angle.

I'd rather just beat the snot out of something than deal with all this accuracy bullshit.

"If you know, then why do you keep doing it?"

"Maybe because a crazy Scot is trying to make a pair of boots out of my hide?" He shot his father a roguish grin. He loved sparring with Gregg, both with weapons and with words.

"Concentrate, son. Keep your lead weapon up and give me a counter with a *stocatta lunga*, followed by a *reversó*, and finish with a *tondo* with your dagger."

Aidan went through the motions of the counter attack with a quick lunge and a low thrust under Gregg's larger broadsword and actually managed to nick him. He quickly flicked the blade of his seventeenth century Italian rapier in a left to right sweeping motion, followed by a horizontal slashing cut of his dagger. Gregg easily parried his moves before they each returned to guard.

"Not too bad, but your forms could be stronger. Why is it when you're bouting with Quinn or Sasha, you seem to have your head completely in the game, but when we focus on forms and precision, you fall apart?"

"I don't know," Aidan said. "I guess when we're just messing around it feels more like fun and I don't have to think about it, but as soon as you start studying my every move it feels like work."

"Aye, you're over-thinking it, son. Eventually you'll fall into perfect formation when you hear the words, and it will feel more natural. It just takes practice and patience, of which you have very little."

"Yeah, but a day off every once in a while might also do the trick." Aidan reluctantly adjusted his stance to continue.

"You'll have time for that when you're older. This period of your life is vitally important to your survival. Aidan, I—"

"You need some new stories, Da."

"Give me ten more minutes and we'll finish up with a

chat." Gregg lunged his attack. Aidan quickly moved to reprise, blocking the huge broadsword with his dagger.

"Do not lead with your dagger!"

"I know!" Aidan growled as he launched into a counter attack. Something happened as he gave himself over to the fight. His focus narrowed and only his next move mattered. The sound of his father's voice faded, except for his booming commands for the forms he expected Aidan to follow. Aidan fell into those forms without a thought. As he moved, he was nothing more than muscle, sword and sweat. His body reacted with perfect precision, his power burning hot in his chest. He'd entered some sort of elevated state of mind where nothing else existed beyond the fight. He was brawn and reaction. Something new was emerging and it scared the hell out of him.

I need to tell Jin about this. Aidan's progress was something he felt more comfortable discussing with his mentor, Jin Jing, but he wasn't certain how to explain this new development. He felt like a machine with little emotion—empty and methodical. But one thing was certain, whatever this trance-thing was, Aidan was sheer perfection!

"Excellent!" Gregg lowered his weapon and Aidan had to resist the urge to take out his enemy when his guard was down.

Da's not your enemy, idiot! Get a grip!

"You're not so bad yourself, old man." Aidan forced himself to act normal.

Do you even know what normal is? In the seven months since his Awakening, he'd changed so much he didn't really know who he was anymore.

"You alright, son? Your eyes are blazing. It's good that you can embrace your power when you fight. Not many can do that and maintain control. Even fewer at your age. But I don't want you relying on it. If you were cut off—"

"I know. I need to be able to perform just as well without the advantage my power gives me," Aidan said nervously. He was having trouble reining this thing in.

"How was your first day back?" Gregg moved to stow his weapon in the glass cabinet along the wall. He showed no indication that he realized what was going on with his son, but Aidan knew it was almost impossible to hide anything from Gregg. He always seemed to know. But he was also good at giving his children the space they needed to figure things out with their mentors.

"The usual," he said as the sensation finally passed. "Lots of pretense, forced smiles and mindless chatter about inconsequential things. The flood of all their suffering was more than I anticipated. It was a lot harder this time now that I'm manifested." He dropped wearily onto the padded bench and grabbed a towel to mop the sweat from his face.

"You will adapt to your gift, son. You just have to give it time. You'll not always feel so much. As you get older, you'll learn to protect yourself from their pain."

"I just wish I could skip to that part."

"High school was difficult for Darius too, but it got easier after he went on to college. He did better with more freedom. You're a lot like your brother in that respect."

"I think I'm just tired, Da. I can't help but feel like I need an escape."

"I know how important your music is to you, Aidan. And I'm well aware that your studies with the conservatory in Vienna would've happened this year. But you understand, don't you?"

"Of course. I know Vienna could never happen, but it's such an incredible school."

"So is Cologne."

"You're right, and two years is not an eternity," Aidan admitted.

"I know you've had a difficult year, but we have to stay one step ahead. The power you own is vast and you're progressing rapidly. The time you've had to heal has been a setback in your training. But you're back on your feet now, so you know what that means."

"More training?" Aidan felt the familiar panic clench his chest. He wasn't sure how much more he could take.

"Your seventeenth birthday is less than six months away. You'll be experiencing a great deal of progress in the coming months and we have to make sure we're constantly testing your limits."

"So what's the plan?" Aidan sighed in resignation.

"You'll begin meeting with Jin for a two hour session before school, three times a week. You will also extend your weekly sessions with everyone by one hour. You need more time with all of your teachers."

"What about football practice? And orchestra?" They weren't much, but they were the most normal things he had. He wasn't ready to give up either activity yet. He'd always known he might have to choose one, but there was no question which he would pick.

"We will continue to work around your schedules as we always have. At least for your junior year, but I cannot promise you won't have to choose next year.

"Good thing I don't sleep much." Between school,

football practice, rehearsals and now extended training sessions, he didn't have much time left for resting.

"It won't always be this difficult," Gregg said. "Eventually you will reach your Proving and you won't have to work quite so hard to maintain control of your power. And then you can have a life." He smiled, but it didn't reach his eyes. He hated this almost more than Aidan did.

"I can handle it, Da."

"You still aren't sleeping well? I thought that was getting better."

"I'm just never comfortable and it's hard to turn it all off."

"It should be getting easier by now. Sasha was restless for the first few weeks, but she's found what works for her. Maybe you just need a little more time than most? That seems to be your M.O."

"Are you saying I'm slow?" Aidan asked dryly.

"Nah. You're just stubborn, lad. Now come on, I have a few surprises for you." Gregg's sudden grin was contagious.

"New weapons?"

"Just a prototype for now." He led Aidan over to the glass cabinet where he pulled two wicked looking, curved daggers from the case. The blades were rather long and the weighted pommels could easily be used as a blunted weapon.

"They're beautiful." Aidan stroked the razor sharp edge of the blade.

"We've been training with the Italian rapier and dagger for a few months now, but I'm not convinced it's the right weapon for you. You were better with the quarterstaff when you were little, but you haven't faired as well with anything we've tried since. Your natural inclination to lead with your dagger tells me you might be more comfortable with dual blades. But check this out." Gregg snapped the daggers together where the pommels joined.

"Nice!" Aidan reached eagerly for the double bladed weapon, each end curving in the opposite direction. Where the pommels joined, it created a single handle that fit his grip perfectly. He could use it like a quarterstaff, with one hand, while the intricately linked crossing guards would offer him protection.

Aidan twirled the weapon, going through a few practice elements to get a feel for its range of motion. It was familiar, like the quarterstaff, but the diversity of the weapon would bring a whole new level to his training. Aidan couldn't contain his grin when he saw how easy it was to separate the blades in mid-motion.

"Good job, old man!"

"The length is modeled specifically to your height and wing span, so it should feel like an extension of your body as you move."

"I'm over Italian swords, Da. Let's focus on this for a while."

"Aye, we'll give it a few months and see what adjustments we need to make but I think this will suit you better."

"It does feel more like me."

"Now, on to your second surprise. Come with me." They left the gym and made their way down the hall. "Starting next week, you will begin training Chloe." Gregg stepped into the small office that Aidan's older siblings, uncles and aunt used when they visited.

"Huh? Why would I train with Chloe?"

"Not with, son. You will be teaching her."

"What?"

"This will be your office."

"No!" Aidan refused the set of keys his father offered. "Absolutely not! I'm no teacher! I can assist, but I'm not—I have nothing—" Aidan's power boiled up inside him.

"Calm down, son. Take slow, deep breaths."

"Da! I'm only sixteen!" His voice broke in frustration.

"And Chloe's training will be part of your training," Gregg said. "I know you're young and I hate doing this to you, but your friends already see you as a figure of authority. They have since you were small children. They naturally defer to you and you don't handle it well. In the not so distant future you will be a very young man with a great deal of responsibility, and you must be able to lead."

"That prophecy is not about me!"

"Whether it is or isn't does not matter. You will always be surrounded by those less powerful, and they will always see you as either a threat or a leader. You must learn to command that authority now while you have the opportunity to do so with someone who looks up to you like a big brother." Gregg's tone indicated the topic was not open for discussion.

"What's wrong, little bro? I heard your screeching down in the kitchen," Darius said as he sauntered into the room.

"Don't you have some detective work to do back in the city?" Aidan snarled at his older brother.

"Pawned it off on my partner. What's with crabby

pants?" he asked Gregg.

Aidan stood, clutching the edge of the desk with white knuckles as he struggled for control.

"He's not thrilled about training Chloe."

"Are you really surprised, Da?"

"Did you bring Kate with you, son? Your mother will want to see her," Gregg asked, giving Aidan a moment to catch his breath.

"Kate broke up with me again. I figured I'd get out of Dodge while I had the chance."

"What did you do this time?" Gregg asked.

"I have no idea. Apparently I'm an 'immature-butt-munch'—her words. And I'm 'driving her batshit.'" He shrugged. "That's what I get for trying to date so far out of my generation."

"You can't deny she's got a point," Aidan interjected.

"Better now, are we?"

"Yeah." Aidan let out a shaky breath. "So, it's just once a week with Chloe, right, Da?"

"Yes. We'll try it for a few months and see how it goes."

"I don't need an office."

"Take it." Gregg handed him the keys.

"Give it to Dare." Aidan shook his head.

"I don't need it," Darius said.

"No, I don't—"

"Aidan," Gregg reproached.

"Just let me use your gym when I work with Chloe. I don't need this. It's ridiculous."

"Darius and the boys can use my office when they're here. I want you to have a place that's just yours. An escape. Somewhere you can do your brooding where I'll know you're safe," he added.

The room was furnished with a large desk and a sectional sofa at the center of the room. Two sets of doors flanked the fireplace; one led to a gym, the other to a private room.

"This is especially for you." Gregg opened the door. "I've asked Darius to soundproof it while he's here."

"It'll just take a minute and a little wave of my mojo." Darius waggled his fingers.

Aidan stepped through the door and knew he'd lost the argument. He couldn't resist the little music studio, complete with a piano and recording equipment.

"There's a small bedroom at the back where you can spend your waking evenings, when you wish."

"You play dirty, Da." Aidan sighed as he accepted the keys to his very own office.

FOUR

"What's for breakfast? I'm starving." Allie yawned as she wandered into the kitchen. Her typically unruly hair was an absolute disaster from a less than restful night. These days she just couldn't seem to turn it off. As she reached for the coffee, she caught her mother's eye.

"Uh oh, I know that look."

"I'm sorry, Allie-girl," Lily said.

"Nuh-uh. No coffee, no talkie." She held up one finger as she poured her coffee and reached for a doughnut. She added a second one to her plate because apparently it was going to be a two-doughnut kind of morning.

"Alright, I'm ready."

"A colleague called while we were away," Carson began. "I've been invited to participate in a research program at the University of New South Wales in Sydney."

"At least it's not too far," Allie said. "But what about

your work, Ma?"

"I can finish from Sydney." Lily pasted on her platinum-fake smile.

"I'm still going to Bali to see Joss, right?" Her sister was completing her residency at a hospital there and Allie was looking forward to spending a few weeks with her. Their parents were actually going to let Allie homeschool for the next term so she could spend some much needed time with Joss. Well they *were* going to let her, but somehow, she knew even those plans had changed.

"Joscelin's going to come visit us in Sydney," Carson said.

"No Bali beaches? Why not? I was looking forward to warmth and sunshine and you know, actual summer in the summer."

"With the move, I just don't think it's a good time," Lily said evenly and Allie knew better than to push.

"Boo! I'm more bummed about no Bali." Her shoulders sagged in defeat. "When are we leaving?"

"Tomorrow," Carson said. "I'm sorry, honey, but it'll be a quick move this time, so pack only what you can't live without."

"My sculptures? Really, Dad?" She stomped her foot in frustration. That's what sucked the most about moving. Most of the time they only took what would fit in their suitcases.

"There's a gallery in Wellington that might be interested in them," Lily suggested.

"Aw, Ma, they're just junk." Allie spent most of her time lately making sculptures out of things she found. She really didn't want to leave them behind.

"They're beautiful, honey."

"Isn't it in your mom contract that you have to tell me everything I make is beautiful?"

"Yes, but in this case, it happens to be true. I showed one of your smaller figures to that gallery owner—"

"At that cool urban place?" Allie gasped. "What did she say?"

"She loved it! We'll stop by later today and see if she's interested."

"Cheers to that! If I have to leave them behind, I'd rather leave them in a gallery than on the curb. I'll have to sort through the garage and see what I have."

"Go get packed first," Lily reminded her.

"Ugh! Packing!" Allie eyed the last doughnut, but thought better of it. "It's so hard to choose what to take and what to leave behind."

"I'm sorry, Allie. I know this isn't easy; especially changing schools again." Carson had a tortured look on his face.

"I don't mind, Dad. Really." She paused behind his seat to drape her arms around his neck. "Changing schools is no big deal. It's the all the packing, moving and unpacking that I'm not a fan of." She wrinkled her nose.

"Well, you're all set up to homeschool this term, so why don't we just stick with the plan and you can start fresh the following semester once you're settled?"

"That would make all of this moving hardship a lot easier to bear." Allie attempted to keep a straight face.

"You're laying it on a bit thick, kid. I could change my mind if you aren't careful."

"Later, Dad. Homeschooling's a great idea!" Allie bolted for her room to pack.

"This is where we're living?" Allie wandered around the tiny, sparsely furnished apartment. The move happened so fast, her head was still spinning from the whirlwind packing and traveling.

"It's just temporary, we'll get something closer to campus once I get things settled with the university." Carson glared at the depressingly small apartment. "At least it has a great view."

"It's beautiful!" Allie gazed across Bondi Beach. "And the beach is within walking distance, not too shabby for Allie. It would be better if it was a warm Bali beach, but it'll do. I'm going to check out my room." She grabbed her meager belongings and headed to the smaller of the two bedrooms.

They had lived in some strange places; like the tree house in Brazil, and the bungalow on the beach in the Philippines, but this was by far the crappiest place ever.

"What are we doing here, Carson?" She heard her mother's voice through the cheaply constructed walls.

"He asked us to come, Lil. It's been years since we've heard from him, but I wasn't surprised. It's nearly time."

"It's strange, so many things happening all at once when we've had nearly two years of peace," Lily said.

"Was it really her? Back at the house?" Carson asked.

"You know it was."

"She was early. By several months."

"I know," Lily sighed. "I'm afraid we've just hit warp speed."

"But you did everything as planned?"

"Of course."

"Then all we have to do now is wait."

Allie's heart thudded in her chest as she quickly

unpacked her speakers and docked her ancient, pre-wifi-iPod. She selected a random playlist to drown out her parent's voices. She wanted to run into their room and ask them what they were talking about. Demand answers to a thousand questions she didn't even know how to ask, but Allie knew it was pointless. She learned a long time ago there were certain questions her parents would never answer. Her intuition screamed for her to ignore it, and experience told her that anything overheard was best left forgotten.

FIVE

AIDAN:

"Chloe, if you say 'yes sir' one more time, I'm going to drop kick you across this gym!" Aidan paced along the padded mat, desperately trying to think of something— anything to teach her.

"Sorry!" she giggled.

"No, I'm sorry. I have no idea what I'm doing."

"You're doing fine, Aidan." She twirled her quarterstaff like an expert and hopped off the four-foot beam with a little flip.

There wasn't a single thing he could teach her that she didn't already know.

"I know can fight with this thing like a pro, but I'm fifteen now and I'm speeding nine-hundred miles an hour toward my Awakening and I don't know squat about anything else. And no one seems to think it's important to teach me anything new."

"We all felt that way, Chlo. You'll be fine."

"Everyone is so busy with you guys, sometimes it feels like I'm slipping through the cracks. More than ever now with Graham's Awakening coming up in a few days." A flash of resentment crossed her face and Aidan could feel how much she struggled with her uncertain future.

"I know it's gotta suck to be the last one." He patted her shoulder.

"It's my turn, now. This is my year and I want to make the most of it, but it's just so lonely all of a sudden."

"I know what that's like."

"Right. You had Sasha and Quinn after you manifested and you had me and Graham before."

"True, but there's always been a wall between me and the rest of you."

"Aidan, I know I've been weird since your Awakening."

"I understand, Chlo. I promise I won't hold it against you." He winked. After he came into his power, Chloe had a hard time being herself around him.

"You know we all respect you so much." She was so earnest, she had no idea that her "respect" was the problem.

"I know. I just hope you realize I never expect your deference. I know your instincts tell you I'm some sort of authority figure. Just don't ever forget I'm your friend first."

"Of course, Aidan. I'm sorry I never really thought about what it must be like for you. I guess that's why you can be so stupid-reckless?" She shoved him playfully.

"Yeah, I guess the isolation makes me a little crazy sometimes."

"I know how much you hate the way everyone reacts

to your power, but don't push us away. I can't stand the thought of you feeling so lonely when we're all right here."

"Thanks, Chloe." He didn't have the heart to tell her that no matter how much they cared—no matter how hard they tried, he still felt alone, like he was on an island by himself and the whole world was just out of reach.

"Well, I don't want *you* feeling lonely or left out. So let's make the most of our sessions. It's time I actually taught you something useful."

"Like what?"

"Well, since I'm not known as the most responsible sort, how about I teach you some stuff the others wouldn't even think about till after your Awakening?"

"Ohh! Like fun stuff?" She bounced on her heels in excitement.

"Maybe. Go on, I'll meet you in the Yard in a minute, I just need to grab something."

He rummaged through his desk until he found what he needed and raced off to join Chloe. Now that he had a plan, he was looking forward to the rest of their session.

He found her waiting in the tall grass near the brook on the edge of the small forest. The Yard still amazed him, even though he'd practically grown up in the underground. He and Sasha played there as kids. They would lay in the grass with Gregg and watch the hazy clouds he shaped into funny faces and figures for them. And if he tried really hard, Aidan could see the stone ceiling just beyond the "sky." Even as a small child, he was powerful, but he never realized back then that he was seeing through his father's gift. Back then, Gregg was their all-imposing father. He still was in Aidan's estimation, but in a different way.

"Alright, Chloe, you ready?"

"Let's do it!" She was so excited about the prospect of doing something new, he didn't want to disappoint her.

"We're going to practice listening."

"Oh." Her smile wilted.

"Come on, it'll be fun. I promise."

"Why listening?"

"After your Awakening, your senses will be in overdrive. It feels like total chaos and it's the worst part about the beginning. But I'm wondering if someone as powerful as you could get something of a baseline of control formed before your birthday."

"You think I'll be powerful?"

"I'll let you in on a little secret, Chlo. You're going to be a tiny little badass, even if you do manifest as a scholar."

"How can you tell so soon?"

"I can feel it." With most kids her age, it was difficult to know what to expect of their Awakenings. Sometimes, like in Aidan's case, the child was so strong, the parents knew what was in store. With Chloe, it was a bit of a mystery. They still didn't know if she would take after her scholarly grandparents, or if she would be powerfully gifted like Ming and Jin. But Aidan could sense her power in a way most people couldn't yet. She would be incredible, either way.

"You're really kind of amazing, Aidan." She gave his hand a gentle squeeze. She was more comfortable with him now than she'd been in months.

I should have taken the time to set her at ease a long time ago.

"So what am I listening to?"

"Here, put this over your eyes to help you focus." He handed her the scarf he'd found in the desk he still hadn't cleaned out. "It's important that you're constantly aware of your surroundings," he continued as she adjusted the blindfold. "Sometimes the smallest detail can be vitally important, so you'll need to recognize the tiniest whisper of sound. But you also need to be able to identify it. Your hearing isn't enhanced yet, but you'd be surprised how much you can actually hear if you just focus."

"'K, what do I do?"

"Relax. Clear your mind of all the mundane distractions floating around and just listen." Aidan watched as Chloe concentrated for several long moments and he was happy to see her taking this seriously.

"Okay." She took a deep breath. "I hear the babbling brook, the birds chirping and something humming."

"We'll come back to that humming sound in a second, but focus on the obvious first."

"Well I hear your breathing and..." Chloe floundered for a moment as she tried to concentrate. "I hear the grass crunching beneath us. I hear something moving. It's faint but close. I think it's your hair blowing in the breeze. You need a haircut," she giggled.

"Hey! I like it. It's low maintenance."

"Mortals don't hear things like that, do they?" she asked in awe.

"You're not mortal, Chlo. You aren't manifested either, but that doesn't mean you can't do extraordinary things. Let's keep going. What else do you hear?"

"That humming sound again. It's like a fan, maybe?"

"Remember where we are."

"Is it the air conditioning?"

"It's the ventilation pump that makes it feel like we're outside."

"That's it! It's a hum with a sort of sucking sound too."

"If Quinn ever figures out his latest gift, he might be able to replace that for us," Aidan said.

"There's a fluttering, thrumming sound too. It's very close, but I can't place it. It's rhythmic and steady, like a heartbeat?"

"Like maybe my heartbeat?"

"Oh! Wow! How can I hear that?"

"You're more powerful than you realize, Chlo. At fifteen, progress happens so gradually it's hard to notice, but it's there and it will get stronger every day. Reach further. Look for sounds you don't recognize."

"There's a sort of churning noise and I'm not sure where it's coming from. It's everywhere, all at once."

"Alright, work it out. If we were actually outside, sitting on a grassy hill what would you expect to be everywhere at once? Something you know is there but you don't always see?"

"Uh ... I don't know. Bugs, maybe?"

"Exactly! It's the insect life teeming all around us. After your Awakening, you will hear dozens of different sounds in that one noise. It's freakishly loud."

"Do you think if I practice enough my senses will be stronger than most Immortals my age?" Chloe asked.

"It's possible. We'll try sight and scent too. It will be interesting to see if this makes a difference for you in the first few weeks."

"Let's keep going!"

"Try to identify the sounds beyond the Yard. I'm curious to see if we can find your threshold so we have something to measure your progress by."

Chloe took another deep breath and focused. "There's something coming from your office but I can't make it out. It's not voices. Is it music?"

"Good one! But can you tell what's playing?"

"Um … no," she laughed.

"Kreisler's *Liebeslied*. What's next?"

"There's a creaking noise. Like an old house settling."

"It's the weight of all that stone and water pressing in on us. It's a good thing your parents keep all that where it's supposed to be."

"Do you think I'll get any of their elemental gifts?"

"Concentrate, Chlo."

"Oh, right. Um, I hear something across the Yard. Voices, but there's a metallic clang in the background."

"Sword fight?"

"Yeah, that's it!"

Aidan lifted the blindfold from her eyes.

"Nice job."

"That actually felt like progress! And it was fun too!" She beamed up at him.

"We'll keep working on it. Why don't you spend some time down at the marina this week to practice?"

"Okay. And I'll keep a journal and we'll go over it next time. Thanks for not putting me through the same old crap."

"I'll come up with some interesting ways we can test what you can't hear and next time I'll be a little more prepared."

"Am I dismissed?" she asked.

"Yeah. Same time next week."

"Wanna go get coffee? You know, now that you're not my teacher."

"I still have another hour with Jin."

"Well, come meet us later then. And hey, Aidan," she said as she turned to leave, "you're pretty good at this."

〜〜〜

As the last strains of Dvořák's *Humoresque* slowly faded, Aidan dropped his bow to his side.

He and Wendy practiced during their free period on Fridays and he always looked forward to it. She was a great musician, one of few who could keep up with him.

"How do you do it?" She shook her head as she settled back in her chair; her cello resting comfortably between her knees.

"Do what?"

"Make it look so easy and effortless. It's annoying!"

"Back atcha, babe." She really was that good, he loved watching her play and he knew she worked like a beast at her craft.

"We have enough time to run through the *Chaconne* one more time," she suggested.

"I'm always up for Bach." Aidan tucked his violin under his chin and began to play.

Wendy was a welcome distraction these days. He could always count on her to get lost in the music with him, and there was something reassuring in the knowledge that she had zero interest in him outside of friendship. She maintained her distance and liked to keep it about the music, which was fine with him. Aidan loved having someone to talk shop with.

About halfway through the sixteen-minute piece, a

couple of giggly girls burst into the practice room to watch Aidan. He rolled his eyes as they continued their mindless chatter.

"Out!" Wendy finally barked at the girls. "This isn't boy band rehearsal! Out!" she snarled without missing a beat of her bow.

"Friends of yours?" She glared at him after they finished.

"No, but can you follow me around and do that?"

"You're a strange guy, McBrien. I see you flirting with those girls in the courtyard like it's your job and you love it. You goof around with your football friends like a total brainless goon. And then you come in here and you're all serious and broody and you play that fiddle like you were born with a bow in your hand and you can't be bothered with that crap."

"Your point?"

"It's like you're two different guys, it just doesn't make sense!"

"I'm this guy, Wen."

"So what's with the BS flirty crap?"

"I flirt because it puts an end to it faster. If I didn't play along with the stupid banter, I'm afraid of how I might really react. I don't want to be rude."

"Dude, you need a girlfriend. Like, a real one. Not one of those vacant-eyed little twits you date for a week before you dump them."

"They usually dump me."

"Really? Let me guess, you act like a total jackass until they've had enough?"

"Pretty much."

"You need someone real, Aidan. Someone like

McKayla Pierce. She's sweet, she's pretty and she has an actual functioning brain. You're already friends, it's no secret she kinda likes you, but at the same time she's not obsessed."

"No way." Aidan shook his head. "We've been friends since elementary school. I don't want to screw that up." Kayla was different. He could be himself with her in a way he couldn't with most girls—even Wendy.

"Eh, you probably will."

"You find yourself amusing don't you?" he asked dryly.

"Aidan, you're miserable here. You can't tell me that Juilliard or The Royal College in London wouldn't just die to have you."

"I was accepted to the Vienna Conservatory. I would be starting next month, but my parents refused to let me go and the offer was taken off the table." He couldn't tell Wendy all the many reasons why he couldn't possibly go to Vienna.

"They won't *let* you? Are they nuts?"

"They want me to wait until I finish high school."

"Mine too, but *Vienna*? It's a dream school!"

"I know, but I was also accepted to the Musical Conservatory in Cologne, Germany. And they're willing to accept me after I graduate. Mom and Dad glommed onto that right away. I tried to talk them into letting me go this year for their preparatory program for gifted high school musicians, but they're insisting I finish school here."

"Aidan, that's incredible! Schools like Cologne don't extend open offers like that! Especially for violinists! They want you as young as they can get you. This is a good thing, you dingdong!"

"I know, but now would be so much better."

"Well, at least you were accepted. I've been waitlisted at The Royal College and Cologne for the last two years in a row," Wendy sighed. "I even started learning German on the off chance I might get a call."

"Hey, you have what it takes. You just have to keep trying. No matter what they say."

"Thanks, Aidan. Besides, they'll have to pry this bow out of my cold, dead hands before I'll ever give it up."

SIX

Allie stepped onto the elevator, loaded down with art supplies and sketchbooks. She pressed the button for the lobby with a deep sigh. It would be a long, frustrating ride down from the seventeenth floor.

Why does this bucket of bolts insist on stopping at every freaking floor?

Allie was sufficiently dressed for the chilly July afternoon, but the sunshine was calling her name. She could have been in Bali by now with her sister, Joscelin. Bali, where it was warm all year round.

"Stupid Southern Hemisphere!" She flung her scarf around her neck and tucked it close to her ears. Several loose copper curls escaped immediately, but she ignored them; anxious to get to the park to check out the skateboarding ramps and do a little drawing.

"Ah, crap." The ancient elevator screeched slowly to a stop on the twelfth floor with a loud hiss. The doors finally creaked opened and an overly tanned guy with fake blond hair stepped inside. He pressed the button for the lobby and rolled his eyes as the doors creaked shut and they started moving again.

"This thing's a total death trap!"

"I got on a few floors up about an hour ago." Allie chanced a joke.

"You're new on seventeen, right? I'm Eric, from twelve."

"Allie." She reached for his offered hand. It was definitely going to be a long ride this morning. She watched as Eric visibly shrank from her touch with a shudder.

"Will you be going to Cook Park High?" he asked, looking anywhere but at Allie.

"Not sure yet. I'll probably wait to start back next semester," she replied as they squeaked past the ninth floor. They came to another juddering stop on the eighth for no apparent reason.

"My floor." He dashed out in a rush to put some distance between them. "See you around sometime," he called over his shoulder just as the doors slid shut.

"Yeah sure," Allie muttered.

He lasted a whole four floors.

Allie took her time wandering through the park, looking for just the right view. She finally chose a spot near the skate park and spread out her blanket in a bright patch of sunshine near the ponds. She quickly had her sketchbook in hand with an array of pencils around her as she got to work. Allie watched the group of noisy guys doing tricks on their skateboards and started to sketch out the vague shapes of their movement. The tallest boy captured her attention, the way he moved gracefully, crouching low to gain speed before leaping into the air, grasping his board on the way back down. She'd tried snowboarding on her recent skiing trip and loved it. Allie felt the urge to join them, but she knew that would only end in disaster.

Inserting her earbuds, she searched for just the right music to fit her mood and settled on Edvard Grieg's *Peer Gynt Suite*. Allie's pencil flew across the page and just as the strings joined the winds at a pivotal moment of *Morning Mood*, she was interrupted.

"Mind if I join you?" the tall, lanky boy asked with a grin. He was cute, with sandy blond hair and friendly blue eyes.

"Sure, go for it," Allie said without removing her earbuds. She started the track over, wanting to hear her favorite part without interruption. She didn't expect him to linger long.

"Man, that wind is cold, yeah?" He sat down practically in the middle of her bubble. "Sorry, I don't mean to crowd you but you've found the warmest spot in the park."

"You're not a bother." Allie forced a polite tone but she kept her eyes glued to the drawing in front of her. She started the track over, trying not to lose her very short temper. She was in the zone and when Allie was in the zone, she didn't like to be disturbed.

"You from Sydney or just visiting?" He was trying very hard to engage her, despite her every effort to discourage him.

Aren't headphones supposed to be the universal sign for 'not available?' Apparently skater boy didn't get the memo.

"Long term visiting," Allie said as *Anitra's Dance* began to play. She'd completely missed *Morning Mood* and *Aase's Death*.

"I'm Gavin. I live just across the park, near Bondi Beach." He gestured with a trembling hand. "If you're new here, you should come up to Towra Point with us sometime. We're always up there kayaking when the weather's nice, and someone's almost always having a bonfire party."

"I'll keep that in mind," her tone softened. He was more persistent than most and she didn't want to be rude.

"Were you drawing us?"

"Oh, um. Yeah. You know the movement really grabbed me. That and the shapes of the ramps." Allie clutched her sketchbook to her chest, eyeing him warily.

He's way too nice. What's the catch?

"Can I see?"

"Oh, no. I—it's just a quick doodle."

"Come on, freckles. Let me see?" He looked at her in a way that made her heart hammer in her chest. She reluctantly released the death grip she had on her sketchbook.

He's so going to get the wrong idea!

"I hate to break it to you, but this is not a doodle. This is me, yeah?" He eased back on the blanket as he flipped through the pages.

"Yeah, uh-you move more gracefully than the others. So it ah-makes it easier to draw you in motion."

"I blame my mother for torturing me with dance lessons until I was thirteen. Wow, you're really good! Can I have one?"

"They're just sketches." She shrugged. "Take whatever you want."

"So you could do better than this? Make it look even more like me?"

"Yeah, with a little more time."

"Will you? Do a drawing?"

"Sure." She didn't know what to make of his eager interest.

"In exchange for a lesson?"

"Oh, no! You don't have to do that."

"You were watching us like you were dying to try it. It's fun and you look like you could use some fun."

"Well … maybe." Allie really wanted to accept his offer. She glanced at Gavin. He was obviously wary of her, but he was still nice when most people would have given up on her by now.

"Don't go anywhere," he said. "Let me get rid of the guys and then we'll have a lesson, yeah?"

"Um … okay."

"It's a date, then. What's your name, freckles?"

"Oh. Uh … Allie." She found herself beaming up at him. She hadn't anticipated he would make the leap from a skateboarding lesson to a date so quickly. Or seem so excited about it.

"Wow, that smile made me forget what I was doing."

"Hey, Gav! Come on!" one of the other boys called.

"Be back in a few, Allie. Seriously, don't go anywhere." He turned and jogged back over to his friends.

Allie, what did you just get yourself into? She slipped her earbuds back in place and settled on Puccini's *Turandot*, beginning with her favorite *Nessun Dorma*.

She eased back into her drawing, sketching fast as she enjoyed the rich color of the violin solo.

"Sorry, I seem determined to interrupt your music," Gavin said.

"Come have some hot coffee with me," Allie offered.

"Oh, you're a lifesaver! I'm freezing!"

"You do know it's really not that cold, right?" She poured the rich, dark coffee into the thermos lid for him.

"We don't do cold here. Wait till December when it's sweltering hot and you're absolutely dying while us Aussies are barely sweating."

"Well, we move a lot, so it's entirely possible I might miss out on summer this year."

"That would suck. The you leaving part." He clinked his plastic cup against her thermos.

"Cheers to that." She smiled, unable to fathom how he was still interested. Allie listened as Gavin chatted nervously. He was making an effort to set her at ease, and for once, she fought the overwhelming urge to bail. Gavin was really nice, and if it was even a slight possibility that they could be friends, she wanted to give it a chance.

"Alright, Allie, I believe it's time for our lesson." Gavin stood and held out his hand for her.

"But I haven't drawn anything yet." Allie was reluctant to take his hand. She was afraid it might burst the pleasant bubble they were in.

"We'll call it a down payment on my drawing."

"But—"

"Do I have to teach you how to have fun? You're kinda small, I could easily throw you over my shoulder." He grasped her hand and pulled her up. He felt it—that thing that made people uncomfortable, but he didn't seem to mind.

"I believe the word you're looking for is short." She eyed him playfully.

"Eh. I'm just crazy tall, yeah?" He winked as they strolled up to the ramps hand in hand.

"So how hard does this suck when you fall? I did okay on a snowboard, but I'm thinking the concrete's not as soft of a landing."

"Falling definitely sucks, unless you know how to fall. We're just going to try skating in a straight line today. None of the big girl ramps or tricks yet. Not until you've got some kneepads and a helmet."

"I'll bring a helmet next time," she said without thinking. She didn't mean it to sound like she was fishing for a date, but he seemed to take it that way and he seemed thrilled about it.

"Perfect! So today, we'll practice starting, stopping, turning, speeding up and slowing down. And if you're good at that, we might try some of the kiddie tricks later."

"Unless I face plant, which is more likely."

"Come on! Let's give it a go, yeah?" He tossed his board down and stepped on, gliding slowly beside her. "Hop up here with me, Allie." He pulled her up beside him before she could blink.

"Ohh, no! Not like snowboarding!" She almost fell, but he held her tightly until she regained her balance. "Got it! Sorry! Don't mind me, I'm a spaz!"

"That actually worked out better than I expected," he laughed, his hands still firmly at her hips. Good thing you have small feet, there's just enough room for you up here."

"Barely." She felt his chest against her back and took a shaky breath. This was way more than she bargained for.

Don't start crushing, Allie. That never works out well for you!

"I'm going to get us going, and then I want you to practice turning. Lean forward to go left and back to go right."

She almost lost her balance again when they started moving faster, but she did as he said, leaning into the turns.

"That's it! You got this!"

"Well, I have a feeling you're doing all the actual work and I'm just standing here. We'll see how it goes when I'm up here by myself."

"You're doing good. Want to try one of the newbie ramps?"

"Sure, let's do it!" She was feeling adventurous and didn't want their afternoon to end.

"Hang on tight. I don't want you to go flying. We're going to speed up a bit and when we hit that dip ahead, bend your knees as we go into it and straighten your legs when we start up the other side."

"Got it!" She eyed the shallow, wide dip in the concrete ahead.

"Here we go." Gavin increased their speed and held her tightly against his chest. As they rolled into the dip, Allie bent her knees. She felt completely out of control when the board went flying up the other side and they landed on two wheels going much too fast. They tumbled into the grass and Allie landed on top of him.

"That was awesome!" She beamed down at him. "Thanks for breaking my fall."

"You can fall on me any time you want, freckles." He reached up and tucked a stray curl behind her ear. "I had a feeling we'd end up in the grass eventually."

Her heart was like a jackhammer in her chest as she scrambled back to her feet.

This is the most fun I've had in a long time. Her vacation with Carson was great, but this was different. This felt like a date. *He's so freaking nice! Don't screw this up, Allie!*

"Want to try it by yourself?" He slid the skateboard over to her, taking a step back. He wanted to put some distance between them, but it didn't feel like the usual rejection.

"Maybe next time. Thanks for the lesson!" Allie really—really liked Gavin and for the first time in ages she felt like someone might actually get her.

"Let me give you my number." He took her simple flip phone and called himself so he'd have her number too. "We're all going to the movies later this week. You should come with us and then we can have another lesson after. I'll bring another board and some knee pads."

"Maybe." She wanted to say yes, but the thought of going with a group made her even more nervous.

"Or you and I could just go together." He seemed to understand her reluctance. "Call or text me anytime."

"I will." Allie smiled uncertainly. She really wanted this to work. She could hole herself up in her room like she usually did, or she could put herself out there and have a little fun with someone who actually wanted to spend time with her.

55

Allie eyed her phone on her nightstand. She'd resisted the temptation to text Gavin for nearly twenty-four hours, but she couldn't stop thinking about him. She was scared and excited about the possibility of a normal friendship with a great guy. Gavin had put the ball in her court but she wasn't sure how to make the next move.

She stared at her phone, trying to find the right words, and then her fingers took over and she hit send before she could change her mind.

Allie: I think I still owe you a drawing.

Gavin: I owe you a real lesson first :) Meet me at the ramps tomorrow afternoon?

Allie: What should I bring?

Gavin: Just you and maybe your sketchbook. I might feel a bit posey ;)

Allie: K see you tomorrow:)

Allie didn't know what to think as she set her phone back on her nightstand.

Do I have a date? Like a for real date?

"Oh crap! What am I going to wear?"

SEVEN

"McBrien!" Jason called across the locker room after their first football practice. "Hey! I'm talkin' to you!" He snapped his towel to get Aidan's attention.

Aidan snatched the towel out of the air and shot him a glare. Jason was like a lost puppy sometimes, the way he followed Aidan around. He considered them best friends, which Aidan appreciated, but Jason really only knew, Aidan-the-jock.

And he would probably revoke my jock card if he knew I was ignoring him in favor of Puccini's Turandot. He tugged on his earbuds.

"What?"

"I'm having a party at my dad's penthouse tonight. You coming? Mallory Jenkins will be there."

"Yeah, sure." Aidan rushed to finish changing. He had just enough time to get home for training. He was absolutely exhausted, starving, and couldn't give a crap about Jason's drinking parties or whoever the hell Mallory Jenkins was. He would have to make an appearance, but he wasn't in the mood to go alone. He reached for his phone and texted Wendy as he headed home for a few hours with Emma and Jin.

Aidan: Please tell me you'll come to a party tonight and keep me out of trouble?

Wendy: Anya will have my head if I don't spend some time with her. Sorry, babe, you're on your own tonight. Think you can manage without me?

Aidan: I'll try. Give Anya a kiss for me ;)

Wendy: She'll be thrilled.

※～※～※

"Dance with me, Aidan?" Mallory attempted to pull him onto the tiled dance floor of Jason's rooftop palace.

"Maybe later, sweetheart." He headed to the bar for another beer, ignoring her gasp of indignation.

These parties were always difficult for Aidan. On the surface, everyone was in high spirits—and some actually were. But he could also feel the stress and anxiety from those on the fringe; the outsiders looking in, desperate to belong. It was a major downer. But everyone expected to see him at these things, playing his role as the cocky arrogant, but popular jock. It was odd how they all wanted him there, but very few made an effort to include him. Aidan gazed around the lavish party at all his privileged "friends." Sure, he never wanted for anything, but he also had responsibilities these guys would never have to face. It left him feeling so much older than his sixteen years.

If they only knew how easy they had it.

"Hi." Kayla sighed miserably from her perch along the parapet.

"Hi." Aidan raised his bottle to clink against hers. She was in a funk tonight, like her heart just wasn't in it, but she'd been feeling down a lot lately.

"You think these guys will ever grow up?" She gestured at the crowd. "Ever realize there's so much more going on around them than these silly parties?"

Her words echoed his own thoughts, making Aidan take a second look. She wasn't just in a funk. Kayla was hurting, but she had her guard up.

"With their endless trust funds and free rides for the rest of their lives, probably not." Aidan's reply could have included both of them, but he had other priorities and Kayla had drive.

"Crappy night?" she asked.

"Maybe not as bad as yours."

"Boys are stupid, and I shouldn't let one ruin my good time."

"You're right about that." He felt his spirits lift. Kayla was always good at making him feel normal. She'd done a study abroad program for most of last term and they hadn't reconnected since she got back. The time away seemed to have matured her.

"Come on, McBrien. I've had a lousy night and you're the best dancer I know." She grabbed his hand and towed him onto the dance floor. She felt his intimidating presence, but McKayla never let his power get to her.

"He's dancing with *Kayla*!" Aidan heard Mallory's hiss of disgust.

"You know, girls are kinda stupid too," he muttered as he held her close, her long blond hair brushing his hands

asked out of curiosity.

"Not important. He's just having a rough time of it and doesn't have a clue how much of a giant D-bag he's been lately." She gazed across the rooftop at Vince, who was busy dancing with some punked out college chick with silvery blond hair and way too many piercings.

"Vince?" *Is he the one responsible for her situation?*
"You can do so much better, Kayla." The guy was a furious ball of rage and hurt. There was so much grief in his life, Aidan couldn't even bear to be around him. He'd lost almost everyone he cared about all at once.

The timing would be about right. One friend comforting another and nine months later—BOOM. Kayla's coming home from some "study abroad trip." He wondered if Vince even knew.

"Thanks, Aidan." She smiled as the hurt look in her eyes vanished. "You have a way about you, don't you?"

"I don't get it!" Mallory gathered her minions around for support. "Kayla's a nobody."

Aidan shot Mallory a scathing glare, grateful Kayla couldn't hear her rude remarks.

"Help me out with something?" As the music slowed, he pulled her close.

"Sure, what's up?" She rested her arms on his shoulders with only a slight tremble.

"Help me deal with that?" He nodded toward Mallory and her friends.

"She does seem determined to catch your attention tonight, doesn't she? What'd you have in mind?"

"Let's get rid of my problem, and make your guy a little jealous." He went in for the kiss, expecting it to feel awkward, but it wasn't. Not by a long shot. Holding

Kayla in his arms, he brushed his lips against hers, tentatively at first. When she let out a little gasp of surprise, he just went for it. It was all really, really ... nice. There weren't any rockets going off, but he could definitely get used to making out with Kayla. Aidan let the kiss linger on much longer than he intended, enjoying the feel of her silky hair trailing through his fingers.

"Well, that was interesting." Her face was flushed as she pressed her forehead against his.

"Not what I expected either." He pulled her closer and kept them swaying with the mellow bluesy song that spoke of soul mates and destiny. It was rather ironic and he almost laughed, but Aidan caught the subtle shift in her demeanor. They were regarding each other in a different light than they ever had before.

This will never be anything deep, but maybe something easy and not too serious is exactly what we both need.

"I always thought kissing you would be like kissing a brother." She relaxed in his arms, letting her gentle teasing banter alleviate some of the tension between them.

"Oh? So you've thought about kissing me, huh?" He smiled, his lips grazing her cheek.

"Well, you are kind of pretty to look at."

"And?"

"Not like a brother."

"But not like douche-boy either?"

"No, not quite, but you'll do in a pinch."

"Back atcha, sweetheart."

"Hey look, your problem is hanging out by the bar with Jason."

"Well played, Pierce," he said dryly.

"Anytime, McBrien. Gotta run, I've got curfew soon.

Thanks for the dance and all the kissing!" She waved as she walked away, completely comfortable with herself and absolutely confident in who she was and what she wanted, despite the rough year she'd had. That was the difference between girls like Kayla and girls like Mallory; you couldn't fake that kind of confidence. Yes, his nearness unsettled her, but she still managed to be herself with him and that wasn't something most mortals could do.

Hell, that's not something many Immortals can do. Maybe it could work, Aidan headed back to the bar for another drink.

⌣⌣⌣

His good mood left with Kayla and after several beers, Aidan realized he might actually be a little drunk.

Maybe the night's not a total waste. Too bad it'll wear off faster than I can blink. Getting drunk-drunk was not an easy thing for Aidan to accomplish—but not for lack of trying.

"McBrien!" Vince called loudly across the dwindling crowd. "We're leaving! You coming?"

"Nah, I gotta catch a ride with Sasha soon."

"Dude, you're coming." Jason pulled him up from the deck lounge. "You have the best fake ID and we need more beer. I'll take you home later. We'll 'borrow' my dad's boat. This party's moving to the beach!"

"The beaches are closed this late."

"Yeah, I wonder how we'll ever figure out how to crawl over that complicated gate thing." He rolled his eyes.

"So we're trespassing? Alright, count me in, but I'm driving, give me your keys." He didn't want Jason behind the wheel. His friend was way too drunk. But no matter how much Aidan consumed, he would always drive better than most mortals could sober. Grabbing the rest of a six-pack, he headed out with Jason and Vince.

"Hope you don't mind, but I'm pretty sure I'm hooking up with Mallory tonight," Jason said.

"Have at it, man. She's not my type."

"While you're at it, you're welcome to take Brianna off my hands," Vince added. "She totally ruined what I had going with Ella."

"That Ella chick is seriously scary, dude."

"I know, but she's crazy hot. Our families go way back, but she's into some weird shit, so that whole thing was on its way out anyway. Dad would flip if I got sucked back into all that."

Aidan ignored their mindless chatter as he thumbed through his playlists.

"No violin crap in my car," Jason said.

"Driver picks." Aidan landed on a rather intense version of Vivaldi's *Four Seasons*.

"I suppose I can live with that. It almost sounds like it's from this century."

Aidan cracked open another bottle as he drove carefully over the bridge into Ohio City to the small liquor store that never asked too many questions. Granted, Darius made excellent fake ID's that were pretty much the real thing.

"I'll go in, you guys just stay here." Aidan slammed the car door as he ran into the store where he felt the unmistakable presence of a familiar Immortal.

Shit! I am so dead!

"Just me, kid," Greyson said softly. He stood at the

register paying for three chilled bottles of Sauvignon Blanc. His tuxedo was rumpled, his white shirt open at the neck and his long dirty blond hair hung loosely down his back—a relic of the ancient past. Greyson Hauser was an Art History professor at the Cleveland Institute of Art and he was normally a really cool guy. But he also worked closely with Aidan's father who was curator of Medieval Weaponry at the Cleveland Museum of Art, which meant Aidan was in it deep. He and his friends were allowed to come and go like any normal kids their age, but they weren't supposed to be wandering around the seedier parts of the city alone. He was supposed to be with Graham and Quinn tonight.

"Should you be here? Alone, no less?" Greyson asked.

"No," Aidan sighed.

"I trust you'll go home immediately and not ruin my date by making me take you there myself?"

"Yeah," Aidan gave another sigh.

"I hate to be that guy, but I have to call your father. You of all people know better, Aidan." Greyson stepped out into the night to slip into his expensive German car with darkly tinted windows.

Aidan grabbed a case of Newcastle and quickly checked out. The cashier was oblivious of the quiet dressing down he'd just received and didn't question his age.

"Let's go boys!" Aidan called cheerfully as he pulled out of the parking lot. He ignored the first two calls from Gregg and then turned the ringer off after the third.

I'll deal with you later, Da. He flipped through his playlists and settled on something loud with an electronic beat.

Cracking open a fresh bottle, he headed for Edgewater Park.

If you're already in trouble, at least make it worthwhile. He stepped on the gas.

"Aidan m'boy!" Jason urged him on. "It's about time, dude. You've been in a funk all night!"

"Hey, slow down." Vince rested his hand on the dash.

"Faster, McBrien, I'm anxious to get in the water with Mallory before she has to go. Sorry man, but you had your chance and you blew it hooking up with McKayla Pierce of all people!"

"I happen to like Kayla," Aidan said coldly.

"Well, you can like her from a distance," Vince said. "She deserves better than an asshat like you."

"I think you're the one that's been an ass where she's concerned, but I'll agree with you for once. I'm definitely not good enough for her." Aidan screeched to a stop near the park gates.

He really doesn't have a clue about what she's been through! He's too caught up in his own shit to see how much she's hurting.

The others were already there, but no one was actually in the water yet. It was a dumb idea for a lot of reasons, but most of them were there just to drink and hang out on the beach.

Aidan felt that overwhelming impulse to find a distraction. Something—anything to make him forget his crappy life for a while. That behavior always got him into trouble, but since he was already in trouble, he just didn't care.

I'm in dire need of a little fun.

"Come on, guys!" He vaulted over the gate and

shrugged out of his shirt and shorts. "It'll be too cold to swim soon. Let's go!" He scrambled along the rock jetty and dove into the cool, black waters of Lake Erie.

Maybe I'll just swim home. It wouldn't be the first time and it wasn't that far, but the mortals would freak out. He could hear them splashing and playing around in the shallows near the shore.

He wanted to let loose with his full capability, but he held back. He rarely got the opportunity to push himself outside of his regular training. Sometimes he thought he could do so much more than his teachers would let him. He felt the urge to experiment tonight.

With a deep breath, he plunged into the next wave and dove deep, down to the rocky bottom of the lake. He followed the slant of the shore until it broke off into a sharp drop. The current caught him there and it was wicked strong as it pulled him down further. It was ice cold and black as night, but he had nothing to worry about. He drifted along with the undercurrent until he was in desperate need of his next breath. Kicking his feet and taking long, powerful strokes, he fought the iron grip of the rip tide and broke free to the surface. He took a deep shuddering breath, drawing cool, refreshing air into his lungs. He stretched out on his back and floated, a huge smile on his face. For the first time in ages, he felt good.

And then he heard the screams.

Shit! He turned back toward the shore, gliding through the water like a fish. Everyone was scared and in a total panic.

I should have felt it!

"Aidan!" Vince shouted. "Do you have him?" His face

was ashen in the pale moonlight.

"Who?" Aidan slowed his pace; grateful that Vince was so distraught he hadn't noticed how fast he was moving.

"Jason! He was following you and he went under. I can't find him!"

"Where did you see him last?"

"Over there!" He pointed to where Aidan was when the current grabbed him.

NO! Fear coiled deep in Aidan's belly. Of course Jason had followed him.

"Who knows where he is now! You should know better than to swim out this far! It's dangerous!"

"I'll find him, just go back to shore and call for help!"

"I'm not leaving till we find him!"

"Suit yourself." Aidan dove below the crest of waves.

I have to find him! Jason was always trying to keep up with Aidan and the other guys on the team but he was usually the one that got hurt.

Aidan paused, drifting along in the cool darkness, but there was no sign of him anywhere. He started to panic. Lake Erie was the shallowest of all the Great Lakes, but it was the most dangerous. People drowned in it every year. The currents ran strong, just below the surface and they would pull you under as quickly as any undertow in the ocean. He'd just been caught in one himself, but Jason wouldn't have the strength to fight it.

Where is he? Aidan needed another breath. He lunged for the surface once more to find Vince still on his tail.

"GET OUT OF HERE!" Aidan roared with all the authority of his power in his voice.

"He's going to drown if we don't find him!" Vince

argued.

"You look over there. I'll look this way." They bobbed in the waves until Vince finally agreed to split up. Aidan turned to swim further out. If Jason was caught in a rip tide, he could have been swept away from where Vince saw him last. Aidan headed in the direction of the current he could feel just beginning to tug at him again.

"Focus, Aidan!" He reached out with his gift, searching for any emotion or pain Jason might be feeling.

Nothing.

Finally, he saw him; hanging limp and drifting along too quickly with the current. Aidan kicked after him, swimming as fast as he could. When he had his arms around him, he lifted Jason's face above the water, but he wasn't breathing. Aidan used his gift to expel the water from his lungs. With a cough and a sputter, Jason gasped for breath and then totally freaked out.

"Don't touch me!" His voice came out with a croak. "I saw you! Nobody moves like that!"

"Easy, let's get you back on dry land."

"Let go of me!" He could see it in his eyes. Jason didn't understand what he saw as he followed Aidan into the depths of the lake. His mind couldn't make sense of it.

"Relax." He reached for Jason with a practiced hand. Aidan let a surge of his healing power flood his body to calm him, and then knocked him out with a single blow. With a strangled protest, Jason slumped over and Aidan headed back toward the shore. Jason trembled and shivered as his body temperature fell dangerously low. Aidan concentrated on making his heart pump regularly, getting the blood flowing through his veins to warm him up. The deep waters were like ice even in summer and

Jason's body couldn't take it. Aidan was tiring quickly with the use of his gift. He was just too young to be of much help.

"Thank God!" Mallory rushed out to help them stumble to the shore. Jason had roused, but he was incoherent.

"YOU JACKASS!" Vince's fist slammed into Aidan's jaw with a loud crunch. Aidan stumbled back into the water with a splash.

"You never think! You know he always follows you and gets in over his head because he can't keep up!"

"I'm so sorry, Jason." Aidan took a step toward his friend.

"Get away from me!"

"You almost got him killed!" Vince slumped to the ground. He was trembling and white as a sheet. "And me too. I didn't think I was going to make it back."

"Why didn't you go for help?" Aidan rested his hand on Vince's shoulder to check his vitals. He was exhausted and cold, but he was okay.

"I didn't trust you to find him. You don't care about anyone but yourself!"

"WHAT?" Aidan lunged at him with clenched fists. *I suffer in silence with them every single day, trying to do what little I can!* Vince's words cut him deeply. To say he was selfish was the lowest possible blow.

This gift ... it's too much. I can't bear it and this overwhelming solitude. How much can one person take before they explode?

Aidan heard sirens wailing in the distance and knew they'd all be in trouble for trespassing.

"Everyone get out of here! Now!" He would take the

blame for this. He watched as the others bolted for their cars, leaving Aidan alone with Vince and Jason.

Gregg's going to go ballistic this time! He'd risked the lives of two of his mortal friends and that was something the Governor would not tolerate—either of them. Aidan scrambled for his clothes to find his phone and dialed quickly.

"Darius? Dude, I'm in trouble."

EIGHT

Allie's phone buzzed in her pocket as she grabbed her peppermint mocha from the barista.

"Hang on!" She juggled her coffee and her phone as she headed for an empty table to wait for Gavin.

"Hey, Ma. Sorry!" She managed to get the phone to her ear before it stopped buzzing. "I left early so I could meet Gavin before school."

"It's alright, Allie-girl, but I have a surprise for you!" Lily sounded excited. "I'll come meet you in a bit."

"Sure, I'm just at the coffee shop on the corner. Take your time."

"Work on that history assignment until I get there."

"Yeah, sure, I'm right on that," Allie said. "What's my surprise?"

"You'll see."

"You know I have no patience for such things."

"Learn some," Lily said sweetly as she ended the call.

Allie sat back in the booth and rifled through her bag for her sketchbook.

The Pharaohs aren't going anywhere. History can wait a little while.

Allie slipped her earbuds in and flipped through her drawings of Gavin. After a lot of sketching, she'd landed on one she liked and was almost ready to let him see it.

She was anxious about their date later that evening. They had plans to hang out with his friends after school. In the last month, things had gone really well between them—when they were alone. Not so much when his friends were around. He was very patient with her and didn't seem to mind whenever she had an awkward moment, but she found his friends exhausting.

"Your drawing skills have improved considerably. I am impressed." The voice was familiar. One she hadn't heard in years, but she knew who it was before she even looked up from her sketchbook.

"Navid!" Allie shrieked when she turned to find him with Lily. "What are you doing here?" She scrambled to her feet and threw her arms around him. He hugged her tightly and swept her around in a circle. Navid never treated her like a pariah. She used to think her touch startled him. If it did, he hid it well, but he seemed like a man who held many secrets.

"It is so good to see you," he murmured as he set her back on her feet. "I'm afraid I am the reason your family is here in Sydney. I'm teaching a short series of lectures at the University and I'm also working on an important project that I desperately need your parents' help with."

Navid was an old family friend and he'd been a

constant in Allie's life for as long as she could remember, but his work responsibilities had kept him absent in recent years.

"I'm so happy you're here! It's been so long!"

"I'm sorry to have taken you away from your school in Wellington. I know it's difficult for you to start over."

"It's alright, I'm used to it."

"I'm going to let you guys catch up." Lily turned to go.

"Thanks, Ma!"

"You must be starving. Your mother said you left before breakfast."

"I'm always hungry these days."

"Not unusual at your age." He winked. Navid was an attractive Middle Eastern man, but he spoke with a very proper British accent. His almond shaped eyes were an odd shade of green that stood out sharply against his beautiful olive complexion. His unruly, dark curly hair was threaded with silver, despite his age. He was several years younger than her parents, possibly late thirties or early forties, but he seemed much older somehow.

Probably because he's so smart. And she knew, the way Allie always knew these things, that he was experiencing a riot of emotions: anxious, a little sad, proud and deliriously happy all at the same time. She could see it all swirling behind his eyes. She couldn't explain it. She just knew it was there.

"Do my ears deceive me or are you listening to classical music at a deafening level?" His eyes twinkled with mischief.

"Yes. Yo-Yo Ma plays Saint-Saëns' *Carnival of the Animals*. And I like it loud." Allie reached for her headphones.

"I'm partial to *The Swan.*"

"I remember. You used to play it for me when I was little."

"Shall we go get some breakfast? There's a great diner nearby."

"Oh, um. Do you mind if we wait a bit? My er— boyfriend-type-person is stopping by before school."

"Boyfriend-type-person?" He arched his brow playfully.

"Sort of. I think. I'm not exactly sure yet."

"Allie! Sorry I'm late!"

"Oh! Hey Gavin!" Allie stood to greet him.

"Wowsa. You can't smile at me like that, freckles. Not when I have to go to school."

Allie laughed as she casually took his hand and introduced him to Navid. She bumbled through it, not sure if she should call Gavin her boyfriend or how she should refer to Navid.

"Nice to meet you," Gavin said politely as he shook Navid's hand and quickly dropped it.

"We still on for tonight, I hope?" He turned back to Allie.

"Looking forward to it."

"Liar. But, I promise my friends will be on their best behavior.

"Come on Gav!" Eric called. "We're going to be late!"

"Sorry, gotta run. I just wanted to come say hi."

"Hi." She flushed beet red.

"Hi yourself." His grin broadened. "Meet you at the skate park around four?"

"Sure." She beamed as she watched him walk away.

"That poor boy doesn't stand a chance," Navid said.

"He is quite smitten."

"He's nice. Most boys aren't as patient with my awkwardness as he is. Now, let's go get food. I'm dying!"

"Awkward? I would never describe you as awkward." They headed out of the coffee shop together, lost in their reunion. Allie was so happy to see him again. She could talk to Navid in a way she just couldn't with her parents.

"You're family. I'm comfortable with you, but when I'm with kids my age, especially a crowd of them, it's painfully obvious that I'm just not like them. Sometimes I can feel the rejection rolling off them in waves. I just have a hard time fitting in."

"You do not need to fit in with the masses, Alexis Carmichael. You need only to hold your head high and be yourself. If the others don't like it, they can go somewhere else."

"Oh, but how quickly I would be alone," she said dryly as they walked along the busy city sidewalk.

"Just remember, if the boys aren't patient and attentive, then they aren't worth your time or your smiles and especially not your tears. So, what's this date about this evening? There will be friends of his there, yes?"

"We're just hanging out at the skate park tonight."

"And this makes you nervous?"

"I'm better when it's just the two of us. I'm pretty sure his friends wouldn't spit on me if I was on fire." She tried to make light of it so he wouldn't see how much it affected her.

"Just be yourself, sweetheart. You're pretty amazing, you know. If they can't see that, then they're blind."

"Then most of my generation is visually impaired."

"This Gavin boy seems to see you clearly."

"He's been good for me."

"Then I approve."

"Thanks, Navid. I've missed you so much."

"It makes me very happy to see you again. I was hoping we could go to the Symphony or the Opera sometime while I'm here?"

"I'd love that!" It felt like a missing piece of her family had come home and she was looking forward to finally reconnecting with Navid after so much time apart.

🙰🙰🙰

"You finally finished my drawing, but are you ever going to let me actually see it?" Gavin asked as he scanned the horizon for whales and dolphins. They were spending the afternoon onboard his dad's excursion boat, taking in the sites with the tourists.

"It's ready." Allie clutched her sketchbook nervously.

"I'm sure I'll love it."

"I know. I just don't show my art to people very often."

"Am I just 'people'?"

"No, of course not."

"Then let me see it."

She watched as Gavin took his first look at the drawing she'd been working on for weeks. After several preliminary sketches, Allie decided to do a negative drawing where she started with a blank page covered in charcoal, and drew with her eraser.

"Wow, this is amazing!" He turned to sit beside her on the bench. She'd drawn him as she'd seen him the first day they met. He'd just sailed up the steep ramp and turned, mid-air, to clutch his board on the way back down. Her drawing caught him in flight, just before gravity took over.

"This is it, Allie. My absolute favorite part of skateboarding."

"The moment right before the fall? Right before reality brings you crashing back to the ground?"

"Exactly. That's when it feels like I can fly!"

"You like it?"

"I love it. It's perfect, freckles." He leaned in for a quick kiss.

"Hey, look!" Allie pointed to the pod of whales swimming in the distance.

"Finally! I was beginning to think we weren't going to see any!" They stepped up to the railing to get a better look. "Can you see? Or do you need to climb?"

"Don't let me fall in." She perched precariously on the bottom rung of the railing. Gavin held onto her, his chest against her back as they watched the humpback whales swimming along the horizon.

"Now I feel like the one who can fly!" She raised her arms over her head and relished the peaceful moment. For once, it didn't matter that his friends didn't like her. The only thing that mattered was how she felt when she was with him. Navid was right. She needed to stop worrying about other people.

NINE

"You stupid, freaking idiot!" Darius furiously signed for Aidan's bail.

"Go easy on the kid, Detective. He's learned his lesson. We've all done stupid stuff," the arresting officer said with a chuckle.

"This one's at his limit of stupid." Darius smacked Aidan with more force than was absolutely necessary.

"OW!" Aidan rubbed his head. "Can we just go home now, Dare?" He wasn't in the mood for drama.

"You really want to trade me for Dad? Or worse, Mom?"

"Good point." With one call, Darius had the arresting officer bring Aidan to the precinct rather than calling their parents. He was grateful for that, but Darius was giving him hell for his stupid stunt at the lake. Aidan knew how badly he'd screwed up ... again.

"Gregg's going to flip his biscuits this time," Darius fumed. "And I'm not going to bail you out with him. You owe me five hundred bucks too, by the way."

"Five hundred? Don't I get a friends and family discount?"

"Let's not find out. I swear if you become a frequent flyer here, I'll arrest you next time!"

"Don't listen to him, kid," the officer said. "Detective McBrien likes to think he's a hard ass, but his bark's worse than his bite. It was nice of you to take the fall for all your friends."

"What friends?" Aidan asked innocently.

"Right." He nodded. "I imagined all those kids fleeing the park like rats on a ship."

"Not. Helping!" Darius shot a glare at his co-worker.

"How's Jason?" Aidan stepped onto the curb in front of the old building on East 21st Street.

"He'll be fine. I think he's more scared than hurt. And I'm sure that's thanks to whatever you did for him. He should have hypothermia for as long as he was out there. And Vince is just pissed off."

"He's always pissed off. I guess it could have been worse, but I think Jason saw too much."

"Probably not enough to worry about," Darius said.

"You think Daniel will talk to him? Make him forget?"

"Nope. You know the situation has to be dire before he'll step in and mess with someone's memories."

"Even if it means losing a friend?" Aidan was pretty sure Jason would never speak to him again without Daniel's help.

"'Fraid so. Listen, Aidan. I'm the first one to come to

your defense in these situations, but what were you thinking?"

"I wasn't."

"Why do you do this crap? Are you trying to get attention? I would think you'd have learned your lesson by now! Ugh! Now I sound like Dad!" He shivered as if acting like an adult gave him the creeps.

"I don't know. It seemed harmless at the time! Haven't you ever done anything stupid and regretted it later?"

"All the time, but I don't put my mortal friends in danger! They could have died all because you wanted to go for a midnight dip in the lake!"

"I know! Believe me, no one will be harder on me about this than myself."

"It's easy to get complacent about mortality at our age. Once you have a few mortal friends die, death gets a lot more real," Darius said.

"Mortality is real enough to me, Dare. I feel it all around me. Everywhere I go someone's in pain or dying! Their pain is with me every second of every freaking day. Like your officer friend back there."

"What?"

"Stage three liver cancer. Unless he gets a transplant, there's not much anyone can do for him."

"Damn. He's a good cop."

"Too bad I can't do shit to help him."

"It'll get easier, Aidan."

"Will it? Is it easier for you? You're what, nine whole years older than me? That's like a spit in the wind, Dare. Is it easier for you, sensing all the crimes happening around you every day when there's nothing you can do about it? Does a few years practice really make that much difference?" Aidan kicked at a loose chunk of cement in the curb as he walked by, letting it crumble to pieces.

"Now, now. No need to destroy city property," Darius said dryly. "And yes it is easier with nearly a decade under my belt. I still struggle with the knowledge I have and the terrible things I see everyday, but it gets better."

"How pissed is Dad?"

"Oh, I'm not telling Greggory McBrien his son's a moron. That's your job."

"Perfect."

"Little brother." Darius stopped him at the corner. "I know things aren't great for you right now and I know you're lonely and pissed off most of the time. Believe it or not, I do understand. But you've got to stop acting out. It won't always be like this. The next time you're feeling reckless, call me. We'll go do something completely asinine somewhere safe."

"That's a bit of an oxymoron."

"No, you're the moron here."

"Thanks, man," Aidan snorted. "Will you help me tell Dad?"

"Hell no, you're on your own with that. There's only so much responsibility I can take before I start feeling nauseous. Come on, I need a drink before I take you home. You won't be seeing the light of day anytime soon once Gregg gets ahold of you—and God help you with Mom."

Aidan winced at the thought of telling Naeemah about Jason. She would be so disappointed in him for not thinking about his friend's safety.

Darius took him to a dive bar down in the Flats, far away from any of the cop bars he would normally frequent after work. The lights were dim and the seats were sticky, but everyone seemed to mind their own business.

The bartenders eyed them warily and Aidan listened to their quiet debate over which one would have to serve them.

"Unbelievable. Let's just go."

"Pitcher of Guinness and we'll leave you ladies alone." Darius gave his flirtiest wink to win them over.

"I hate to be the one to break it to you." Darius filled Aidan's frosted mug. "But it's my job to tell you when you've been an intolerable ass and it's a job I take seriously. You are a *major* buzz-kill lately."

"Dare, you have no idea what it's—"

"So you're more powerful than anyone in the room, big freakin' deal. You have to own that shit."

"It's not that easy."

"We need to find you some powerful hot young girl who can kick your ass around that gym. That's what you need—hell, that's what I need."

"I wouldn't say no to that." Aidan clinked mugs with his brother. "Just one problem with your evil plan," he said. "I've never met a girl who could even keep up with me in a fight. Except maybe Sasha, but that so doesn't count."

"Well, there's one you're forgetting about." Darius grinned.

"Naomi Hauser," they chorused together.

"But she's teaching in Paris. And she's older."

"She's my age." Darius waived it off. "You know that doesn't qualify as an adult in our world. Do I remotely act like the twenty-four year old narcotics detective I'm supposed to be? Of course not."

"That's 'cause you're twenty-five, Dare."

"Whatever. The point is Mom still seats me at the kids' table with the rest of you. I'm not ready to be a for-real adult, which incidentally, is one of the many reasons Kate kicked me to the curb again. She thinks it's time I grew up, but I don't plan on doing that for at least a century," he rambled on as he poured another round.

"Kate will get over it. She always does."

"Not this time, little bro. She's moving on and I can't blame her. It's time. The age difference is just too extreme with us. I don't know how Imogen and Lucian make it look so easy."

"They're Complements. It's different."

"I don't know. I'm worried if I can't handle a relationship with Kate when there's just five hundred years between us, how will it ever work with my Complement? She's could be as old as Emma."

"Back on the 'she's older kick,' are we?" Darius couldn't seem to make up his mind if his Complement was a lot older or younger.

"I don't know how some people can be so certain. Everything I feel from her is conflicting. Sometimes she feels ancient and wise—intimidating as hell, but other days, she feels distant and vague like she's still really young. It's frustrating."

"Now look who's acting all broody?" Aidan gestured to the bartender for another pitcher.

"It's hard when your generation had the lowest female birthrate in history. There're literally less than a hundred Immortal women my age in the whole freaking world! Two of them are like my little sisters and the only other one I know is Naomi who has the attention span of a gnat when it comes to relationships. It seriously narrows the dating pool."

"So date younger."

"Younger is tricky." Darius sighed.

"Sounds like *you* should give Naomi a call."

"She scares me. And stop head shrinking me! When did this get to be about me, anyway? We're here to make you feel better."

"It's how I roll," Aidan said. "I don't even know I'm doing it anymore. My gift tells me you're upset by the breakup and I have to fix you."

"Focus on yourself, kid. I've survived breakups before."

"I think I just need a change of scenery." Aidan tossed back the last of his beer and poured another. "I've been a total mess since the accident. After all those weeks of regenerating, I still don't feel right. It's like I'm disconnected from who I used to be and I'm just not me yet."

"Regenerating at your age does not happen in a few weeks. Yeah, you're walking and talking and all the visible wounds are healed, but it goes deeper than that. It takes time up here." He tapped Aidan on the forehead.

"I wouldn't wish it on my worst enemy," Aidan said.

"Well, I'm sure I could convince Naomi to come for a visit to cheer you up."

"Probably not a good idea. Mom's not a huge fan."

"Omi does like the McBrien boys," Darius chugged his nearly full glass.

"What are we going to do about you, Dare? No one would fault you for coming back to high school with us.

It would be so much easier on you. I like seeing you like this. You remind me of my brother. Detective McBrien's a total asshat."

"I barely made it through high school the first time. And I had Naomi back then to keep it interesting, with Erin and Mia not too far behind. It wouldn't be the same, but it's a tempting idea. If there were some cute Immortal girls there that weren't like my baby sisters, I'd say sign me up in a heartbeat."

"Cheers to that." Aidan drained his glass.

〜〜〜

"What's the matter with you!" Wendy glared daggers at Aidan before he could even take his seat in the Orchestra pit on Monday. "Trying to drown yourself? Aidan, you're a smart guy but sometimes, you're such an idiot!"

"You done?"

"For now."

"I'm grounded for the foreseeable future. I've been yelled at all weekend and I'd really like to spend some time with someone who doesn't hate me."

"I'll see what I can do. I'm in the doghouse myself, you know."

"What did you do this time?" Wen was always in trouble with her temperamental girlfriend.

"Anya is very upset with me. I've had some rather big news. I'm hoping you'll be happy for me, considering everyone else in my life is less than thrilled."

"What's up?"

"Germany called." She chewed on her bottom lip. "I'm in."

"Wendy, that's fantastic! I'm so proud of you!" He

reached to hug her and suppressed the wave of sadness he felt at the prospect of her leaving—sadness and jealousy. But he refused to let her see that. She was absolutely terrified to go, but he also knew how much she wanted this and wasn't going to make her feel bad about it.

"When do you leave?" He pretended to ignore the way she quickly pulled away. There was no doubt, Wendy cared about him, but she liked to keep her distance. But with her, it never felt like a rejection.

"In a few days! I can't believe this is happening! My parents aren't happy, but they know how much I want this. I thought Anya would understand, but she's not even speaking to me."

"Well, I'm excited for you, but I'm going to miss you. Who am I going to practice with now?"

Unexpectedly, she burst into tears.

"Hey, what's this?" He tried to comfort her, but she waved her hands at him, insisting she was fine.

"Damn it! I hate tears! I'm just so freakin' scared!"

"You'll be great, Wen. It's just nerves. Once you get settled, you'll be in your element."

"What if I'm not good enough?"

"You are the most talented musician I know," he said firmly. "You've got this, Wendy. Don't psych yourself out."

"It helps knowing you'll be there soon. I think that gives me the courage to actually go for it."

"If I have it my way, I'll be there for senior year, and you and I will take Germany by storm."

"Thanks, Aidan. Your support means more than you know."

TEN

"Allie, you should learn to play an instrument while you're young," Navid said. "You have an excellent ear for music and I know how much you enjoy dancing. Music is a part of who you are. It's a cathartic release for you. Look at how much you enjoyed the Massenet Opera last night, and then our evening spent discussing Thaïs." He paused as the waitress delivered their breakfast of eggs and toast, which Allie immediately smeared with Vegemite.

"What?" she asked when she caught him frowning at her.

"I do not think this ... stuff qualifies as food, sweetheart."

"It's delicious!" She added a fried egg to her Vegemite toast, which even Gavin thought was gross.

"I move around too much to even think about taking

piano lessons." She took a huge bite. "It's just not practical."

"Practical? Allie, you're an artist in every sense of the word. I've seen your portfolio. You should be proud of your accomplishments, and you should never stop challenging your creativity. It's as much a part of your education as history and mathematics."

"So maybe I'm just lazy."

"I am merely attempting to point out a minor flaw in your well rounded education. You shouldn't neglect your talent for music because of logistics." He waved his hand irritably. "You stand on the sidelines far too often as it is. You should be a participant in life, not an observer. Don't just listen to others making music. Make your own."

"Oooh, speaking of making things. Want a cookie?" Allie pulled the plastic container from her bag.

"Oh, you baked? Like ... unsupervised?"

"Har har. Look, they turned out beautiful!" Admittedly, she was a disaster in the kitchen, but she was going kayaking with Gavin later that afternoon and really wanted to surprise him with homemade cookies and coffee.

"I followed the recipe to the letter, I promise. Try one."

She watched as Navid took a tentative bite and then his eyes lit up.

"They're good?"

"Delicious. They remind me of my wife's. She was an ... incredible cook." He stifled a cough.

"Your wife? I never knew you were married."

"It was a long time ago. I'm afraid we're no longer together."

"I'm so sorry." Allie reached for his hand as the waitress passed.

"Can I get you two anything? More tea?" she asked.

"Water. Please?" Navid asked.

"Hey, it's Allie!" She recognized Eric's condescending voice and wanted to shrink into her chair and disappear.

"Hey guys." Allie turned to see Eric with his latest girlfriend, Courtney and several of their friends from Cook Park High.

Why do they travel in packs? It always feels like they're ganging up on me.

"Are you ever going to start school?" Courtney asked.

"Probably in a few weeks. I'm homeschooling for now." Allie shifted her gaze to a point just over Courtney's shoulder.

"So, you'll be going to Cook Park?" Eric sounded disappointed.

"Oh-um. I-um, I don't know." Allie glanced down at her feet. "I thought I might like to go to school with Gavin. But, I-uh. I'm not sure yet."

"Wouldn't you be more comfortable at a smaller school?" Courtney asked. "I mean, you've only been dating a few weeks. What happens when you two break up?"

"I guess, I hadn't really thought about that."

"Listen, Gav's a nice guy," Eric said, "but you might not want to—"

"Enough," Navid said softly, but they all heard the steel in his voice. "Leave, now. All of you."

Without a word, they turned and fled.

"Can you follow me around and do that?" Allie attempted the feeble joke, but she was so humiliated.

"Alexis Carmichael, you are always such a confident, self-assured young woman. I do not understand this insecurity." Navid gave her a worried look.

"The self-confidence is a carefully placed illusion. In social situations it tends to crash and burn."

"I'm so sorry, Allie. I had no idea. Why do you think you react like that to them? Or they to you?"

"I don't know." She fidgeted in her seat.

"Be honest. Let's pretend for a minute that I will completely understand anything you say. Get it off your chest, sweetheart."

Something about the look in his eye and the earnest sound of his voice made it all just come tumbling out. "I can *feel* how much they hate me. Those two in particular. Most of the time kids my age just don't get me and for some reason, I make them nervous. So I do what I can to appear less threatening. I'm passive and awkward because I just don't know what to say. You just saw it. I can't be myself with people like that."

"It's worse than I thought," he said. "I suppose you've kept this from your parents?"

Allie nodded. "I've never felt like I could explain it. I'm trying to be myself here, and with Gavin, it's easier. These last weeks in Sydney I've been pushing myself out of my comfort zone, doing things I don't normally do. It's been scary, but it feels necessary. Like I was satisfied with things the way they were for a long time, but it's just not enough anymore." She frowned at her choice of words, but she trusted Navid would understand.

"You're very perceptive, Alexis. You'll be sixteen in a few short months. You are entering a stage of your life when everything can change in the blink of an eye and you must be prepared to adapt. But never change who you are at your core. Do not alter yourself just to gain their approval."

"You're right, I shouldn't let it get to me."

"You've spent too much time alone, sweetheart. This worries me. You need others your own age. People who understand you."

"If there are such people, I've never met them. I'm doing better with Gavin, but even with him it's like there's a distance between us I can't seem to cross. He tries very hard not to let it affect our relationship, but it's an obstacle I just don't know if we'll ever overcome. It's weird. There's just ... something not quite right about me." Allie's eyes filled with tears. This was the closest she'd ever come to voicing these fears.

"Stop," he said firmly. "There is absolutely nothing wrong with you. And I don't ever want to hear you say that again. There are others like you." He reached for her hand. "You're uniquely different in every way, but that is not a bad thing. Embrace your individuality. It's nothing to be ashamed of. The people who blend into the masses—like those nasty little pieces of work back there— they are the uninteresting ones. Those who are brave enough to break the mold are the ones that become the shining stars. Hold your head high and be proud of who you are. If you intimidate them, if they don't like you, so what? It's not your job to make them comfortable at the expense of your own happiness. If Gavin likes you, and you like him, you'll find a way to work around this problem with his friends. And you will do it together. He's been good for you, sweetheart. I just don't know if it's enough," he added softly.

"So you're telling me to let my freak flag fly?"

"In a manner of speaking, I suppose." He rolled his eyes.

"I know you're right. I like who I am, but there's a huge part of me aching to belong *somewhere* in this world. I don't think that's too much to ask." Allie sighed as she watched a group of noisy teenagers at the next table. "Logically I know there's nothing really wrong with me, but it doesn't make it any less lonely."

"You're one of those young women who will thrive in college. I have taught at some of the most prestigious universities around the world, and I've watched countless young men and women blossom before my eyes when they've finally found a home where they are accepted for who they are. Two more years of high school is not an eternity," Navid said. "But at your age, it probably feels like it."

"I don't know, good things are happening here. I'm starting to hope we'll stay in Sydney for a while. I'm just so tired of starting over."

"Don't let the changes life throws at you define who you are."

"Your words are all sound advice in theory. In practice, it is much harder."

"Then we just need to find you an environment where you can flourish." He stood to leave. "Unfortunately, I have a class to get to, but I'm taking another cookie for the road." His brilliant smile lit his face. "Enjoy kayaking with Gavin and at least try to have a good time at the party."

"These people have entirely too many parties." Allie grabbed her sketchbook and followed him out of the diner.

◊◊◊

"Let's go, freckles!" Gavin hopped out of his old clunker of a truck to help Allie with her backpack. "I've been looking forward to the weather breaking for weeks!" It was early August so the evenings were mild now and they were both eager for an afternoon of kayaking.

"We'll have to hike for a bit until we get to the water, but Eric's already got the boats there. It's a little swampy where we're going. Hope you don't mind crocs." He grabbed her hand as they headed along the trail.

"If I see a single crocodile, you'll be seeing a short redhead walking on water, screeching like a howler monkey."

"I'm kidding! They aren't active where we're going. I doubt we'll even see any."

"You doubt?" She shot him a glare.

"If we see any, just ignore them and they'll ignore us."

"That's your sound advice? Ignore them when I look like a tasty snack? I don't think so, Gav!" Allie stopped walking. "I'm serious, if I see anything that could potentially swallow me whole, I might start climbing. And if we're on the water, you'll be the tallest thing out there."

"Relax, I'm totally joking! Crocs don't come down this far south. You crack me up sometimes. I wish you could—" he let his unfinished sentence hang in the air between them.

"Wish I could be more myself with your friends instead of a total weirdo?" Allie asked.

"That's not what I meant."

"It's the truth." She stared at her shoes out of habit.

"Look at me, Allie. I know you have a hard time in a crowd. And that's okay. I just wish they could see how great you are. That's all."

"Thanks. Last time was better, wasn't it?" she asked. They'd gone to the skate park with just a few of his friends and it hadn't been horrible.

"You did great." He took her hand again, lacing his fingers through hers. It still surprised her when he made an effort to be close to her. But it took effort. Even now, she could see how determined he was to walk with her hand in hand. It was nice. But it didn't always feel natural.

"I guess I'm just good at reading a room, you know. I can tell when people don't like me and when I know that, it's really hard to chat and joke around and act like a normal person. I can't be fake about it, so I just look at my shoes instead. I like shoes." She chanced a smile. She didn't want to ruin their time together with this kind of talk. It would only lead to questions she had no idea how to answer.

"Just be you. If that's snarky, smart-mouthed, hilarious Allie, that's awesome. If it's quiet, cute, shy Allie, that's just as wonderful."

"You're good at this." She skipped ahead, dropping his hand to give him a break.

"At what?" He jogged to catch up with her.

"Digging yourself out of a hole," she said sweetly.

"Dammit, Eric!" Gavin darted ahead of her. "He was supposed to take the boats down to the water for us!" Several off-road vehicles were parked in the clearing, but the two-seater kayak she and Gavin would be using was still secured to Eric's truck.

"Hey, no worries. We can get it." Allie scrambled up the side of the truck and unlatched the boat.

She held on as Gavin guided the boat down and she walked it forward. He reached for her end and set it carefully on the ground before he returned to help her down.

"So how exactly are we carrying this thing? We have a differential height situation going on if you haven't noticed."

"Yeah, that's why I'm gonna kill Eric later. Come on, babe, we got this." He hefted the boat up to his shoulder.

Allie grabbed her end and lifted it high up over her head so Gavin could do the same.

"Wait, wait! Too high!" She almost lost her hold. "Okay, got it! Sorry! Pay no attention to the total spaz back here!"

Gavin readjusted the boat back to his shoulder. "Okay, we're never going to get anywhere if you keep making me laugh!"

"I'll be good, let's go!"

"It's not far, freckles. Just down that trail." Gavin set a pace she could keep up with and they soon had the boat in the water.

"Hop in and I'll get us going," he said.

Allie took the front seat and grabbed her paddle as Gavin gave them a push and jumped in behind her.

"Where to?" Allie stared to paddle out.

"See Eric's stupid fake blond hair over there, yeah?" He pointed across the still waters with his paddle.

"Can't miss it." Allie steered them toward the others. "There's a lotta boats out there." There were way more people around than she'd anticipated.

Relax, Allie! It won't kill you to mingle.

"Let's take our time. Eric's been an extra special kind of jerk today."

"Probably my fault. I seem to irritate him with my presence." Allie's paddle sliced through the water matching Gavin's pace.

"Quite the opposite, actually. That's the problem."

"What?"

"For days all we heard about was the hot new redhead up on seventeen." He rolled his eyes. "And how we were all going to be so jealous when he scored with her."

"What a jackass! You do know he actually ran away from me the first time we got caught in the elevator together? I bet he didn't tell you that part."

"Of course not," Gavin scoffed.

"So that's it? He's jealous?"

"Absolutely green with envy. Eric usually gets all the attention."

"Sorry." Allie didn't want to cause trouble between Gavin and his friend.

"I'm not. Eric's not worth it!"

"Well, why don't we check in with your other friends for a bit?"

"You sure?"

"Of course. I don't want you to feel like we can't do things with them just because I get nervous."

"Okay, but we'll take it just a few people at a time." They fell silent as they paddled further out to the first cluster of boats where some of his friends were racing. Allie clumsily chatted with the other girls as Gavin cheered for his friend, Chris, in a race against Eric.

They made their way from one group to another, never staying long enough for Allie to feel self-conscious. They soon found themselves out in the open water of Botany Bay.

"Take a break?"

"Sure." Allie marveled at the wetlands all around them. "It's weird how all of this is so close to the city." She watched the birds flying overhead.

"Let's get you turned around so I can see you." Gavin reached to unlock the swivel on her seat.

Allie drew her knees up so she could turn around without falling into the bay.

"That's better. I have food and drinks if you're hungry." He reached for his backpack. "Thought we might have a picnic."

"Oh! I made cookies and hot coffee!" She reached for her bag.

"You made me cookies?" Gavin handed her a sandwich and a bottled water.

"Yep, and Navid said they were delicious!" She poured them each a cup of coffee from her thermos. "Try one!"

She watched as Gavin took a big bite and all the color drained from his face as he choked on his laughter. The rest of the cookie fell from his hand into the water.

"Oh darn, would you look at that?" He swallowed with a wince. "I seemed to have dropped my cookie."

"Aw, they can't be that bad!"

"Navid was right, they're delicious, babe." He winked. "But I had this really big breakfast."

"Oh." Her face fell. "They're terrible."

"No, not terrible." He shook his head with a grin. "But I'm thinking you might have used a dash too much salt."

"Salt?" Allie took a bite and spit it out. "Seriously? I mixed up the salt and sugar! Ugh! How can I be so bad at something so simple?"

"The coffee's great."

"Oh no! Navid!" She dissolved into a fit of giggles.

"Did he really eat one?" Gavin asked. "Like a whole one?"

"Two! But I'm starting to wonder if they ended up in his pocket!"

"He must really love you."

"I'm going to stick with coffee as my single contribution to the culinary world."

"Good idea." He chugged half a bottle of water to wash the taste out of his mouth.

"You could have spit it out!" she said.

"I didn't want to hurt your feelings!"

"I'm not made of glass, Gavin! Next time just tell me, 'dude, your cookies seriously suck!' I promise I won't break!"

"Next time? How about we keep you out of the kitchen?"

"Probably a good idea."

"Hey! What's so funny?" Chris called across the water.

"Allie's cookies! Try one!" Gavin tossed one at his friend.

"Chris, don't listen to him!" Allie giggled. She glanced around and saw several of his friends watching them curiously. Navid's pep talk came back to her, giving her a little boost in confidence.

"Hey Kelly!" Allie waved. "You guys want to skirt through another canal before we head back?"

"Sure."

"Awesome!" She turned back to see Gavin beaming at her.

"Good job, Allie!"

It was nearly dark by the time they got back to the truck, but Allie was having a great time.

"You ready for the party? We don't have to go if you don't want to." He pulled her close as he leaned back against the truck.

"Let's go, it'll be fun." She let her arms drape around his neck, leaning in against his chest. His hands lingered at her hips as his lips brushed against hers. Allie ran her fingers through his hair and he let out a startled gasp. Kissing Gavin was nice, but the earth didn't shift under her feet. Sometimes Allie worried his feelings were a little more intense for her than she realized.

"Come on, freckles, let's get outta here."

ELEVEN

Wendy: They're going to vote me off their island!

Aidan: Last time I checked Germany was not an island.

Wendy: They hate me! I'm butchering their language!

Aidan: Other than challenging feats of backward linguistics, how's school?

Wendy: Amazeballs!! I cannot wait until you get here!

Aidan: That makes two of us. Any hot girls?

Wendy: Can't think about that now. I miss Anya 😣

Aidan: She was total batshit and you're hot. I'm sure half the music prodigy's are swooning, and the other half are just waiting for me :)

Wendy: Dammit! Now I miss you too! The time difference blows, I have to get some sleep. I have music theory at the crack of dawn.

Aidan: Night, Wen. I'm glad you're doing this. I'm proud of you.

Wendy: Night. Thanks for being in my corner.

Aidan sighed miserably as he dropped his phone. He missed her more than he cared to admit.

He sat alone in his studio in the underground. He was still grounded from his latest antics at the beach, but his mother insisted he be allowed to keep his newfound sanctuary. If for no other reason than to give him time to think about his actions and how it seemed to have permanently affected his friendship with Jason.

Aidan absently hit record, lifted bow to strings and began playing Mozart's *Air*. The achingly sweet melody filled the soundproofed room and his thoughts drifted back to Wendy. This was one of her signature pieces. The subtle nuances of the slowly exaggerated notes sounded forlorn without her cello to accompany him.

Get a grip, Aidan! It's not like she was your girlfriend!

He was feeling lower than he had in months and he poured everything he had into the music, feeling his power smoldering deep within his core. There in the privacy of his studio, he could play in a way that he would never share with another living soul. It was too personal—too raw. Even when he listened to his recorded tracks, he could feel the music filled with his frustrations, fear, anger and all of his self-loathing. It all just came pouring out, like some kind of emotional release. He would play like this for hours and sometimes he felt better, but most of the time, it left him feeling like he had nothing left to give. Then it would all build back up again and he'd be right back here, playing his heart out for no one to hear.

Aidan meandered down the long flight of steps to the stone grotto on the beach. His father had built the grottos for his mother ages ago. There wasn't much Gregg wouldn't do for Naeemah. He did it himself, despite the fact that Ming could have done it in a day. It was a peaceful place where the waves lapped gently at the room's perimeter. The grotto was Aidan's favorite spot on the island. When he was with his friends, he often felt like he wanted to be alone, but once he was alone, he craved people. In the grotto, it was just comfortable, thanks to Naomi's gift. She'd left for Europe more than a year ago, but she was powerful enough to sustain it still.

Everyone was in the underground, sitting vigil for Graham's Awakening. Aidan tried to sit with them, but he couldn't take it. No matter how much he wanted to be there for his friend, it was just too painful. Instead, Aidan spent the day alone. The sun was setting and there would be a celebration soon, but this was one of those nights he felt like an intruder. He synced his phone with the surround sound and settled on something sad and broody to fit his current brood.

He felt so off balance. Like there was a piece of him that still hadn't fully regenerated from the accident yet. That was the only plausible explanation for the funk he'd been in since Tibet. Even in training, he couldn't focus, and Jin spent most of their last few sessions berating him for his lackluster performance.

I gotta snap out of this maddening spiral. He absently stacked driftwood in the fire pit. *I'm starting to annoy myself.* He grabbed a six-pack of Blue Moon from the fridge and settled on the sofa to call Wendy before it got much later.

"Hey!"

"Was gehft?" she yawned loudly.

"Nicht vie—and that about taps out my German."

"You sound broody. Seriously, what's up? Spill it, I'm tired so you have about ninety seconds before I start snoring."

"Were you serious about me and Kayla?"

"YES! She'd be good for you. And I happen to know she likes you."

"She might be going through some stuff right now."

"We're all going through stuff, Aidan."

"True, but what if I screw it up?"

"You probably will."

"Thanks for the vote of confidence."

"It's high school. Lighten up. There's no reason you can't have a healthy relationship with a nice girl without it getting too serious. Just see how it goes. And do not pull that fake Aidan BS with her!"

"I'm going to do it," he said firmly. "I'll ask her out next week."

"Great, just don't be a dork."

"I'm a lot of things, Wen, but I have *never* been a dork."

"That depends on who's asking."

"Gute Nacht, Wendy. Thanks for listening."

"Anytime, babe. Auf Wiederhören."

Am I really doing this? Was Kayla the right girl? He definitely liked her. They could be a good match, but something about the idea just didn't sit well with him.

Aidan stared at the fledgling flames in the fire pit, willing them to catch and burn hot and bright. He frowned as he felt his power stirring when he hadn't reached for it.

"No!" He gripped the edge of his seat as the flames spread and a burning sensation blossomed in his chest. He was losing control. It was slipping away from him so quickly and without warning.

What's happening? Aidan doubled over as the heat spread to his limbs. The fire responded to the power coursing through his body and it began to grow, spiraling into a tall pillar. Hot flames licked at the stone ceiling, leaving trails of thick soot as smoke and ash filled the room.

Aidan collapsed in a heap as every muscle in his body seized in sudden agony. He lay there, unable to move as his power erupted, free and unrestrained. He finally saw it—how insanely powerful he was and how easy it would be to let it rule him. It was tempting, to give into it and fight no longer.

The fire had nowhere to spread in the cold stone grotto as it blazed, white-hot. The air scorched his skin, making it crack and bleed.

He took a desperate breath, clutching his skull as some new facet of his power began to emerge like an alien force ripping from his body. He couldn't move and he couldn't stop it.

It's not supposed to be like this!

He lay there for an eternity, wrestling for control, but feared it was a battle he would lose.

It's the fire! Everything was linked to the fire. He had to put it out, but he couldn't move and he didn't know enough about this newest gift to understand how it worked. The flames roared, billowing up from the pit in the floor. It didn't spread, but grew hotter and hotter until the ceiling glowed.

"Aidan Loukas McBrien! What are you up to now?" His mother burst through the concealed door to the underground.

"Mom!' he cried in relief, his face covered in blood, soot and sweat.

"Aidan!" She was at his side in an instant. She struggled to move him, but that wasn't the answer.

"No! Put it out!"

Naeemah darted into the kitchen, leaping over the sofa to land on the bar. She returned with the fire extinguisher and had the flames out in seconds.

Aidan choked as the last spasms wracked his body. Naeemah reached for him with trembling hands.

"Don't touch me!"

She shivered from the sheer amount of power surging inside him, but she didn't let it stop her.

"It's okay," she crooned in her lilting melodic voice as she helped him away from the fire pit.

"Water."

Naeemah used her gift to call several bottles of water from the kitchen. It was a testament to her worry; she never used her power in the open like that.

Aidan chugged the first bottle, letting the coolness soothe his parched throat, and dumped the other bottle over his head.

"Glad you showed up, Mom." He grasped her hand.

"Deep breaths, son. Find your control." She brushed the singed hair from his face.

"Sorry I torched your grotto."

"Shhh. Aidan, it's okay. Just focus on your breath.

Nice and slow."

"What do you think this is?" He was healing quickly. Much faster than he should at his age, but it would still take days for the burns to fade completely.

"I'm not sure. I have never seen a gift emerge so violently. I've known other young Immortals who have endured pain with a new ability, but never like this."

"Apparently, that's my lot in life," he groaned as he sat up.

"If I could take it all on myself, I would," Naeemah said. "But I promise it won't always be like this. You are strong, my son. It's harder for you, yes, but it will never be more than you can bear."

"I know." He smiled for her benefit. He wished there was something he could do to make this easier on her. She took it so hard whenever he struggled.

"Can you stand?" she asked.

"I think so." But as soon as he did, pain shot through him like he'd been beaten *and* burned. His legs gave out and he stumbled.

Naeemah draped his arm across her shoulders and guided him to the stairs.

"I don't think I can do it, Mom." His body ached with a deep soreness that had nothing to do with the fire and would not heal so quickly. This pain stemmed from his newest emerging gift and he wondered if this would be the one that would push him over the edge.

Can an Immortal lose his mind?

"Lean on me, son. I am strong enough to carry you."

TWELVE

Allie watched Gavin as he joined the other boys for a game of football along the grassy shore of the beach. She should be okay with it, but she felt a wave of dread creep up and all of her insecurities flooded back in to drown her. Even after all these weeks and all the progress she'd made.

You have to learn to function without a buffer! She was doing well interacting with Gavin and his friends these days, but when he wasn't there, she fell apart.

"Hey Allie! Come join us by the fire!"

Allie watched as Kelly and the other girls huddled around the driftwood fire. The cold weather was breaking and the warmer temperatures would be upon them soon.

"I-I ah, I'll join you in a … in a minute. I-I'm just going to get a drink." Allie hated the way her mind went blank in these situations. She had no idea what to say or how to act with these girls and most of the time her words came out in a tumble of stutters. At least Kelly seemed the nicest, Allie just wasn't sure it was sincere.

I don't even want a drink. She usually sipped on the thick dark beer the others seemed to prefer. She didn't see the draw. It tasted awful and it never really affected her. Gavin didn't drink much either, so she followed his lead.

Allie stepped toward the row of open tailgates where the keg was set up. She didn't quite know how to work it and she stared at it for a minute until she heard the other girls laughing. She fumbled with her empty cup and changed her mind, grabbing a fruity, fizzy bottled thing that probably tasted like cough syrup. She reached for a slice of pizza and then she heard them.

"She's so weird!" Leslie whispered, her voice carrying with the wind.

"Does she give anyone else the creeps?" Kelly asked. "I promised Gav we'd be nice, but there's something so off about that girl."

"Do we know what school she's going to yet?" Courtney asked. "It's bad enough now, but I don't want to deal with this crap at school too."

"Come on girls, be nice to the weird girl. Gav's totally smitten," Eric said as he joined them. "Can't imagine why. She's way more trouble than she's worth."

"Poor Gavin," Leslie said. "Do you think he's regretting it yet? He's such a sweet guy to have to deal with all that fumbling and stuttering all the time."

"To be fair, she's not like that with him," Kelly said.

"Well, he's thrilled." Eric shook his head. "That's as close as Gav will ever get to a hot girl."

"Hot? More like a hot mess," Courtney said. "She's

painfully awkward. It's hard to watch. But sometimes I think it's an act to get sympathy. That girl is way more confident than she lets on."

"He insists it'll get better if we're all nice to her," Eric said. "But I tried to talk to her in the elevator when she first moved in and she went mute, wouldn't even answer me. This thing with them can't last long."

"Well, I just don't understand why he has to drag her to our parties when no one wants her around," Courtney said loudly.

Allie dropped her slice of pizza and the bottle slipped out of her hands to crash onto the truck bed. The pizza box fell to the ground and she turned to see everyone staring at her.

"Screw this! I'm done!" Allie fought back tears as she stalked away. She refused to let them see how much their words hurt. She'd rather go back to spending her time alone than deal with such hateful people. *Why did I even bother trying?*

"What the hell's wrong with you guys?" She heard the hurt in Gavin's voice and wished she could have a ctrl+z. This tension between Allie and his friends was making him crazy.

I shouldn't have said anything!

"We didn't know she was listening. Gav, just let her go," Leslie said.

"You're terrible people. I'm ashamed of all of you!"

Allie tripped over the tall grass and stumbled toward the beach, clutching her sweater. She didn't know where she was going, but she had to get out of there.

"Allie! Wait!" She heard Gavin call behind her, but she kept moving across the sand dunes.

"My friends are idiots, Allie. Don't listen to them!"

"They're right! Why do you want me around?" She stumbled in the darkness and fell to the ground. She watched Courtney and the others at the bonfire party below. She could hear their laughter. They didn't even feel bad.

You don't belong down there, Allie. As much as she liked Gavin, she wasn't sure this was ever going to work.

"Gavin, I know how people feel about me, but walking into a heated discussion about how much everyone can't stand me just isn't something I can shrug off."

"I'm so sorry." He sat down beside her.

She absently reached for his hand and felt his subtle flinch; that constant reminder that her touch startled him. He felt the same way they did, but he was willing to look past it to see the real Allie. It meant the world to her, but it just wasn't enough.

I can't go to Cook Park High. It'll never end well. She wanted so badly for everything to fall into place here in Sydney, but the timing was off and it wasn't going to work no matter how hard they tried to force it. Gavin was great, but it was like he just wasn't the right guy and his friends weren't ever going to accept her. But Allie wasn't ready for it to end. Not yet.

"See? You feel the same way." She dropped his hand.

"I do not." He laced his long fingers through hers. Allie appreciated the way he resisted the urge to pull away from her, but she wondered when it would get to be too much for him.

"I'm a pariah, Gavin. I don't know why. People just don't like to be near me."

"You are an intimidatingly beautiful and unique girl."

He brushed a comforting kiss across her fingertips.

"Unique?" she snorted. "That a nice way of saying I'm weird?" She felt more like herself now that they were alone, and that just wasn't fair to him. Why couldn't she be like this with the others?

Because they hate you and you can feel it.

"Okay, you're weird." He grinned. "But hot-weird, which in my humble opinion is an excellent combination."

"Thanks."

"Seriously, don't ever try to be anything less than what you are, Allie. You're different, and that's an incredible thing. You just need to own it."

"You're right."

"Come on, freckles. Can I tempt you with hot fudge sundaes? My treat?"

"Extra fudge?"

"On one condition."

"Name your price."

"Ignore my friends, because you and I are good. More than good." His kiss was tentative at first, but he grew bolder as she responded. He was the first to break away, as usual, but she didn't mind.

"Let's get outta here." He offered his hand. She took it, reveling in the way it felt to be close to someone, but she had a nagging suspicion that everything was about to crash and burn.

THIRTEEN

LILY:

"Why is it when I show up to do the dishes, I find you've already done them?" Carson asked as Lily shut the dishwasher.

"I'm convinced it's your gift."

"The phone was ringing," he said innocently. "Navid's on his way over."

"Do you think he'll finally tell us what this whole jaunt to Sydney's been about? He's been so vague about why we're here." With Allie's birthday looming on the horizon, Lily worried the next few months would be too much for their daughter.

"I think he just wanted to spend some time with her, Lil. It's been years, he doesn't really know her anymore."

"It's sad. They're so much alike. It's been wonderful seeing them together again." She just wished they could have stayed in New Zealand a little longer. But circumstances made that impossible when Livia showed up on their doorstep long before she was expected. It would have been nice to let Allie have her last months of peace in a home she was familiar with, but it just wasn't safe anymore.

Sydney felt like Limbo, even though she'd seen positive changes in Allie since they arrived. She was becoming more adventurous and Gavin was really good for her, but she was headed for such a turbulent time. Lily worried this relationship was all very bad timing. She just didn't have the heart to stop it.

"I'm glad Navid's had this time with her, considering the difficult road we're all facing." Carson's words echoed her thoughts.

"I'm not ready for this," Lily said. "I thought by the time she got to this age that it would be easier somehow, letting her go—to finally be who she is."

"She will always be our daughter, Lil. That's been the most important factor in all of this. It's vital that she identifies as a mortal. Raised by a mortal family she loves, completely ignorant of her heritage."

"I just wish I could make this easier for her. I'm afraid she won't take it well when she has to leave us."

"If I know our daughter, she will throw an epic fit."

"But Navid will be the best person to train her and get her through this," Lily said.

"I know it's only two years, Lil, but I'm going to miss her. I know she needs to be with Navid to train in a safe, remote place, but I can't wait till she's back with us and we can finally go home. I'm ready to get this done."

"She won't be the same."

"None of us will."

A soft knock at the door announced Navid's arrival.

"Here we go." Lily breathed a silent prayer for courage. This felt like the beginning of everything—the end of Allie's childhood, and the dawn of a terrifying, uncertain future.

Lily took one look at Navid's face and knew he'd made a monumental decision about their daughter's future. In their minds, Allie had four parents. They'd always acted together for her benefit, but Allie would be his daughter far longer than she ever would be theirs. Still, Lily couldn't stand not knowing what Allie's future would hold. She knew it was almost impossible for Kassandre and Ashar to see and interpret what would come. Even with their gifts, there was still such a snarled mass of contradictions and unmade decisions ahead of them. She didn't know how they could ever make sense of it all. Lily and Carson's role in this was important, but even they only knew what they absolutely needed to know and nothing more.

"What's changed?" Carson asked as they all took a seat in the living room.

"I'm struggling," Navid said. "I've looked forward to this phase of her life as much as you both have dreaded it."

"You're wavering," Lily said in surprise. Navid was always so certain in the decisions regarding Allie.

"The plan has changed, yes."

"Is that wise?" Carson asked. "We've spent her whole life making these decisions and sticking to them implicitly."

"And our goal has always been to keep her safe and teach her what she needs to know," Navid agreed.

"So why go back on that now?" Lily didn't want to hope for a last minute decision that might keep Allie with them, but her heart was nearly bursting with the possibility.

"She will not be happy. She isn't happy now and she doesn't even realize it. I thought keeping her isolated would be a difficult sacrifice, but that it would be for the best. She has so much time ahead of her. I thought her safety would be worth the loneliness she would experience cut off from our world, but I hoped she would forget it in time and look back on her childhood fondly."

"She is lonely, but I wouldn't say she's unhappy," Lily said. "We'll take her home when she's a little older like we planned. The others her age will still be there when she's eighteen."

"Two years is nothing to me," Navid said. "But it is an eternity for her. Her childhood will be over so quickly, and our daughter will have to fight for her freedom every single day. I thought spending the next two years with me would give her some happiness and allow us to get to know each other, but I am no longer certain that is in her best interest."

"What are you seeing that we aren't?" Carson asked.

"When she was little, I'd look at her and see her vibrant mother. Now that she's older, I see a glimmer of myself there too. But Alexis is dying inside, my friends. And she doesn't even know how to express it. She needs the friendship and the acceptance of her own kind—of her own generation, and she needs it now. Not two years from now."

"How will this affect the rest of her life? Should we not stay the course as planned?" Carson's face grew white at the prospect of making a rash decision.

"This will not change anything significant. She has you both. She doesn't need me. Not now. My daughter and I will get to know each other when she is older. These few weeks in Sydney will have to be enough to sustain me."

Lily felt sorry for him. Navid was like a man haunted.

"So we're leaving?" Lily wasn't sure deviating from their plan at such a critical time was smart, but the thought of keeping her daughter with her a little longer was tempting.

"You will leave tonight. Before I change my mind."

"Wait, we need to talk about this," Carson said. "I need to know that this Governor and their family are the right ones to ... to finish raising our daughter. That was never part of the plan! We always said we four would raise her. That you would train her!"

"You have new jobs in Cleveland. I've had a trusted friend make all the arrangements with Greggory. He is expecting Lily as his new curator of Egyptian artifacts at the Cleveland Museum of Art. He does not know about Allie and he does not know I'm still living. He cannot be told these things. When he sees Allie, he will suspect, but he will not ask too many questions now. Eventually he will figure out who she is, but by then he will be just as invested in this as we are. I always intended for Gregg and his family to train her for her Proving anyway."

"Can we really trust these people?" Lily asked. "What if they try to take her from us? That's the thing we've been running from all these years."

"Greggory McBrien once had a very special bond with Kassandre. We trust him and Naeemah more than anyone else in this world. They will do what is best for Allie.

Their children will be her truest friends. Whether we take her there now, or in two years from now, they will be her family in a way none of us will ever be."

"So are we telling her everything tonight?" Carson sounded terrified.

"We cannot tell Alexis anything." Navid's voice was filled with regret. "She must go into this completely blind."

"Blind? What do you mean, blind?" Lily lurched from her chair. This was news to her.

"This game we are playing with the future. It is not an exact science," Navid continued. "We've always known Allie will be powerful. If an Immortal child is like a ticking time bomb in the weeks leading to their Awakening, Alexis is like an armed nuclear warhead. She cannot handle such a revelation until after she is manifested and has the strength to contain that much power. We tell her nothing."

"Navid! That's outrageous!" Carson gripped the arms of his chair until his knuckles turned white.

"If you tell her, everything will be for naught. This close to her Awakening, the shock would be too much. She would lose control and never become the woman we all need her to be."

"So we take her home and let her meet these people? People who will not know she can't be told?" Lily nearly sobbed. Navid wasn't telling them everything. He never did. She couldn't fathom how she would ever survive this only knowing half the story.

"It's only two months. We should stay here and get her through this before we uproot her again," Carson insisted.

"This should have been our plan all along," Navid said. "I just … I needed her. Or I needed the promise of her to get me through these last years without losing my mind."

"This is too rash." Carson held his head in his hands.

"You have always trusted us. You've always done what we've asked, knowing we could not divulge all the details. I am asking you to trust us again. This is what's best for Allie."

"Where will you go?" Lily knew Navid was right; they'd always done as he asked. She knew Kassandre saw something in their daughter's future that they couldn't know. They had to continue trusting blindly.

"I will live as I have since she was a small child, constantly on the move."

"She will have so many questions. What are we to tell her?"

"Nothing. You must pretend you know nothing. It will be easier for Greggory and his family to leave you alone if they believe you became her parents by mere chance. Which means Allie must believe that too."

"It seems unlikely that he wouldn't come to us when he learns she has been raised by mortals," Carson said, looking for any possible flaws in the plan.

"Greggory is the most patient of men when it truly matters. He will have questions, but he will not leap to ask them. There may come a time when he decides to approach you. If that time comes, I will intercede."

"Navid, she will have no one to confide in," Lily said. She and Allie had always been close. She couldn't abide the thought of how they might drift apart through all of this.

"This is an impossible thing you're asking," Carson said. "I don't know if I can do this to her. Not telling her. Not preparing her. It's like throwing her to the wolves."

"She will rise to the challenge. We must remember, Alexis is strong and stubborn like her mother. When she finally accepts this life, she will *thrive*."

"It's going to kill her to leave Gavin." Lily was afraid Allie would resent them for tearing her away from him so soon.

"She's already questioning that relationship. She senses that it will never work," Navid said. "And there are other friendships waiting for her."

"Is there anything else we should know?" Carson asked.

"No, my dear friends. Your job is nearly done. I cannot tell you anything more than you already know. There is a slight chance that Allie and I will have our own special way of communicating in the years to come. It depends entirely on how her gifts manifest and develop. It won't be much, but it is all that I have to give her."

"How much time do we have to prepare her for the move?" Lily asked.

"Your flight leaves in a few hours."

"Then I need to start packing." Lily squared her shoulders and steeled herself for what they were about to do to their daughter.

FOURTEEN

"I feel like death on a biscuit." Aidan rolled over and stared at the clock.

"Wow, I overslept?" He was groggy and bleary eyed, and his bed looked like a war zone, but for the first time in ages, he'd slept a full night.

Aidan stood with a stretch, but his legs trembled and he stumbled to the floor. Even two weeks later, the episode in the grotto still plagued him. His body ached with a bone deep weariness he couldn't seem to shake.

How am I ever going to get through a whole Saturday session like this?

As he struggled to get dressed, his every move was stiff and slow. He made his way down to the kitchen hoping breakfast would help.

"Feeling any better?" Naeemah asked as he shuffled into the kitchen.

"Yes and no." He poured a cup of coffee, hoping it would give him the jolt he needed to get through the morning. "I slept the whole night, but I'm just not bouncing back."

"Sleep is good progress. How about an omelet? You need the protein."

"With cheese and bacon? And not that turkey crap you keep trying to convince me is food. I'll make the toast, since you have a habit of charring it."

"I do not."

"Really, Mom? You're gonna lie?" Naeemah was a brilliant woman, but when it came to the dinner rolls, they beat her every time.

"Oh fine! Go make your toast! But you're having a veggie omelet with a sprinkle of cheese and make that wheat bread, no butter."

"Aw, Mom! No butter? That's the whole point of the toast!" He dropped the thick sliced sourdough bread he preferred and grabbed the dry-as-sand multi-grain stuff.

No one else has to worry about this crap!

"You look exhausted, son. You slept, but you're not at your best. Keeping your diet clean will only help your recovery."

"I kept my diet clean all summer, Mom. I thought I was done with that! I ate nothing but rice and bland chicken with vegetables for two freaking months!"

"And it helped. It gave you the added strength you needed to heal. It will do the same now."

"It's not permanent, right?"

"For someone like you, a clean diet could be a tremendous help."

"We've been over this! I like my cake, my fried things

and my butter. I deal with a lot, but I draw the line at butter."

"Try it for a few more weeks and then I'll back off. But when you get a little older, it may be inevitable."

"This sucks!" He flopped onto a seat at the bar as Naeemah reached for the gas burner to heat the pan for his omelet.

He saw it all in slow motion: the way the pilot light sparked and the burner flushed with heat; the way the flame rose high as she poured the eggs into the skillet. But it continued to blaze as it responded to Aidan's errant new gift. The fire flickered and flashed, rising higher to spread quickly up her arm, burning through her thin sleeve and scorching her flesh.

"Mom!" Aidan cried as the phantom pain shot up his arm and his power burned deep in his chest.

Naeemah screamed as the unnatural fire engulfed her hair and face. The heat of it hotter and brighter than it should have been. She stumbled to the floor. Aidan moved slowly, as if his limbs were weighted down with cement. He had to stop this!

"Mom! No!" He beat at the flames with a towel, but they kept coming back. She curled up into a fetal position and bit back her screams.

"Aidan! The burner!"

He needed to cut off the source. He lunged for the stove and extinguished the flames. The fire went out with a puff of smoke.

"Mom, I am so sorry!" Aidan sobbed as she lay on the floor panting for breath. Her beautiful hair was a charred mess and her face and arms were blistered and raw.

"It's okay. I'm okay." She winced as she sat up,

clutching her arm. Aidan crouched down beside her and the ghost of her pain nearly overwhelmed him.

"No! This is not okay!" He felt completely helpless when he tried to heal her and nothing happened. He was still too young and his fledgling gift just wasn't strong enough.

"I am fine, Aidan." She swiped his hands away gently. "Do not tire yourself. I will heal."

"But I can—"

"You will not take my pain. It is not so much that I cannot bear it. Save your strength, son. See, I'm already healing on my own." She held her arm up so he could see the fading burns.

"How about cereal for breakfast?" She attempted a grin, but the gruesome sight of her face beneath her charred skin was like a punch in the gut. "And maybe a protein smoothie?"

"Don't joke about this!" He sat down beside her, his face ashen.

"These things happen, Aidan. Please do not blame yourself."

"How can I not? I set my mother on *fire!*"

"And I'm healing."

"This is not okay!" he said again. "I can feel everything I just put you through. Even your fear, Mom! I did that."

"My fear was for you and what I know this will do to you. I am not as old as your father, but I am old enough to know that pain will always pass. It is momentary. When you're older you will understand that there are much worse things."

"Like hurting the people you love the most?"

"Like watching the ones you love the most suffer when there is nothing you can do to help," she said softly. "Help me up. We are putting this behind us now."

"I'm so sorry." Aidan lifted her and set her on her feet. She was much better already. Even her hair was coming back.

Aidan ran his hands through his hair in frustration and reached for his mother. He held her as tightly as he dared, towering head and shoulders over her slight frame.

"It's okay, son. We will figure this one out, just like we always do."

"Da's going to flip."

"He doesn't need to know."

"Like hell! I'm not keeping this from him. I need to get a hold of this thing now!"

"Fine. We'll go talk to him after you've had breakfast." She steered him back to his seat, plopped a box of cereal and a carton of milk in front of him, and left to change her ruined clothes.

Aidan rested his forehead against the cool quartz countertop. He had a huge day ahead of him but he wasn't sure he could face it. Jin would be expecting him soon for their three hour session, and then it would be Ming Lao's turn. After lunch, Aidan would spend what was sure to be another brutal session with dear old Da before ending the day with his mother. He didn't know how he would survive.

∿∿∿

"Ready to get started?" Naeemah asked as she swept into her office.

Aidan barely managed a grunt from where he lay sprawled on her sofa. Blood trickled from his left nostril.

A sign he'd pushed himself to the edge.

Mom won't like that. He wiped his nose, but it was too late, she'd already seen it.

"I will be having a few choice words with your father tonight! What's he done to you? Or was it Jin this time?"

"Both. They're just trying to help me figure this thing out so I don't hurt anyone else. What if it happens again? With someone who won't recover? You know I can't take that risk."

"I told him not to push you so hard! One day's respite after what you've been through will not delay your progress!"

"It's okay, Mom. I'll rest up and I'll be fine in a few days. I've got better control of it now. I just wish I understood this thing. "

"It takes time to know and understand your gifts. You'd think that overbearing old Scot would know that by now. Come on, let's get you out of here." She pulled him to his feet.

"I love you too, Mom." She struggled with his power in a way that his father didn't, but no one could ever say Naeemah didn't love her son. He could feel the strength of it everyday, and he didn't need his gift to tell him that.

"Where're we going?" He winced as they headed to the underground garage.

"I'm taking you to my yoga studio downtown." She helped him into the front seat of her black SUV.

Naeemah drove through the tunnels to the concealed security gate at the back of their property and headed for the ferry dock.

"Are we working out?"

"Absolutely not. I'm taking you to McDonald's, and

then you're going to spend some quality time at the spa. Whirlpool, sauna, massage and then bed."

"If you take me to McDonalds and make me order a salad, we are no longer friends."

"You need calories right now. Order whatever you want."

"Awesome. Can I have extra french fries?" He rested his head against the soft leather headrest.

"I suppose, just this once."

FIFTEEN

ALLIE:

"Ferryboats?" Allie peered through the window as Carson drove onto the docks at Edgewater Park. She eyed the underwhelming skyline of Cleveland, Ohio. "It's so small."

"Cleveland has world class culture." Lily was practically glowing with happiness now that they were finally "home."

"I'll be the judge of that," Allie muttered.

"The Cleveland Orchestra is one of the finest in the world," Carson said.

"So score one for Cleveland. But what was wrong with London or New York? Or someplace exciting?"

"We've spent our lives in the hustle and bustle of the world," Lily said. "We wanted to come home. To show you what you've missed all these years we've dragged you along behind us."

"Don't feel bad, Ma. I happen to like our nomadic lifestyle. It's never been boring. The school changing sucks, but the sightseeing has always been stellar."

"We'll still travel," Carson said. "But now we have a home to come back to."

"Until someone offers one of you the job of a lifetime."

"We're officially retired, honey. This is our home now. I've been offered tenure and Dean of Anthropology at Case Western Reserve University, and your mother will be curator of Egyptian artifacts at the Cleveland Museum of Art."

"So this has been in the works for a while. Why did you let me get so close with Gavin if we were just coming here?" There was so much about this move that didn't make sense.

"This all happened very quickly, Allie-girl." Lily gave a deep sigh of regret. "I would never have let you get so attached to Gavin if I'd known this was going to happen. These opportunities are unprecedented and we just couldn't turn them down."

"I don't buy it. It'll never last." Allie sat back with a huff and gazed across the murky waters of Lake Erie.

"I know we haven't given you much cause to trust us when it comes to moving around," Carson said, "but I promise this is it. I hope you can be happy here, Allie."

"So what's this Kelleys Island place like?"

"Look for yourself." Carson pointed in the distance.

Allie leaned over the front seat and saw trees looming on the horizon. Gulls swarmed overhead and the sun glinted on the tranquil waters.

"It's pretty." *Translation—boring.*

"We grew up here. You're going to love it!" Lily

clasped her hands anxiously as they drew closer to her childhood home.

Allie stared out the window as they left the docks behind and drove through the quaint town square.

"Wait! Where's the rest of it?"

"You can get just about anything you need here on the island."

"So that was it? I'm gonna die here," Allie groaned.

"You can go into the city whenever you feel like you're about to die," Carson said cheerfully. "I'm sure you'll make a full recovery."

"Har har. Hey, what's with the church?" They'd turned down a tree lined drive leading to a rambling stone church with an actual bell tower.

"We're home!" Lily nearly bounced in her seat. "We bought this place a few years ago and had it converted into a residential space. The bell tower is your bedroom. I hope you'll like it."

"The Quasimodo suite? Nice!" Allie got out of the car and stared up at the old building. "It's totally nuts! I love it!"

"Aw, we figured you'd hate it." Carson ruffled her hair playfully.

"Well, you wouldn't be you if you did normal, so I guess if you're gonna be weird, you oughta go big or go home." Allie followed her parents through the arched red doors into their new home. She gasped in surprise when she took her first look at the huge living room with the grand circular staircase. The interior no longer resembled a church, even though most of the existing architectural elements were still intact. An entire wall had been removed and replaced with glass, offering a view of the gardens.

"This is awesome! I don't know what I was expecting, but luxury was definitely not on the list of possibilities!" Allie turned around the spacious foyer in awe.

"The main part of the house has been renovated, but the building across the gardens will be a guesthouse eventually," Lily explained. The entire first floor was one open space with an enormous living room and a kitchen at the rear of the house, complete with glass doors opening onto a small herb garden. The dining room was just off the kitchen in a sunken-grotto-style room, and Carson's study was opposite the living room. A second arched red door led to Allie's quarters.

"This will be your space." Lily opened the door. "Go explore, make yourself at home. We'll be in the kitchen."

Allie took a moment to admire her little living room, minimally furnished with a small sectional sofa, a wall mounted television and another glass wall overlooking the gardens. A covered path ran between her tower and the guesthouse that she didn't think they would ever need since they didn't know anyone.

Maybe Navid will come for a visit?

She darted up the narrow stairs to the bedroom landing where she was greeted with three doors. The door directly in front of her led to the second floor of the main house, the door to her right opened to her tower bedroom, with a terrace balcony, high ceilings and fantastic views through tall windows.

The door to her left concealed her very own master bathroom, with a giant jetted tub and a walk-in closet, already filled with gray and blue school uniforms.

"Surround sound!" Allie did a little dance at the sight

of the speakers recessed in the walls.

From her bedroom another set of steep stairs, like a ship's ladder, rose up to an art studio at the top of the tower. It was completely stocked with everything she could possibly need and she was itching to get started on a mural.

If this really is "home" then maybe I'll paint my studio with images from all the places we've lived! She could see it vividly—the beaches of the Philippines, the tree house in Brazil, the sweet little cottage in Eastbourne and the Sydney Opera House.

Her mind whirled with the possibilities, but she couldn't resist the lure of the last set of stairs leading up to the roof.

"This is so my spot!" She walked onto the rooftop garden. It was sparse, with two Adirondack chairs on a raised deck overlooking the city in the distance. Around the deck, wildflowers and tall grasses grew from the surrounding beds. Lily knew better than to give her any kind of gardening responsibilities. The plants would have been dead within days, but this, the rain could manage.

Allie stepped up to the parapet along the deck and looked down. Her head swirled with vertigo as she peered over the edge.

Whoa, that's high!

As she stood there, she felt like she really was on the edge of something big. So much about this move was different and she wanted to embrace it, but she was terrified of taking such a leap of faith. She didn't want to love this place, only to be ripped away from another home.

"Be cautious, Allie. But don't go back to being that girl

who was too scared to be herself." Allie turned away from the spectacular view and felt strengthened by her little pep talk. Navid was right. It was time she stopped worrying about what other people thought of her. It was time to stop observing and start participating in life, and this was the perfect time and place to make that change.

"That's it then. I'm not going to be a weirdo here." *Well ... maybe just a little bit, just to keep it interesting.*

Allie wandered back down through the maze of the second floor. She passed an upstairs den off the master suite and another home office for Lily right by the staircase, which looked more like a piece of sculpture.

"So who died and left us a fortune?" She joined her parents at the bar in the kitchen. She eyed the polished concrete countertops. Of course granite was much too normal for Lily.

"This is our retirement home. We've been saving for years," Lily said.

"You couldn't tell me about it? I could have helped with the design choices."

"It was for the best," Carson sighed. "Trust us that we've always had our reasons for doing things the way we have."

"Alright, then. What's with the uniforms in my closet?"

"You've been accepted to Cliffton Academy!" Lily was clearly thrilled by the prospect.

"But American schools aren't back from summer vacation yet!"

"Cliffton follows a schedule similar to what you're used to. They've been back in session since July, so you start Monday."

"*Monday*? That was so not on my to do list for the week!" Allie sighed as she trudged back up to her bathroom to test drive the new tub. "I cannot believe I have to do this again."

SIXTEEN

"Jeez, they've really done a number on you this time."
Sasha rushed to help Aidan into the living room.

"Yeah." He winced as he settled into his favorite
armchair. "But this doesn't feel like overtraining. It feels
like my Awakening in slow motion."

"I can't believe they've got you training through that!
That's not cool."

"If I don't get a grip on this fire thing now, it will only
get harder to control."

"Come on, you need to eat," Sasha insisted.

"I'm not hungry."

"Liar. Don't go getting all broody about this, little
brother. It will pass."

"I know, but if the casualties start piling up, I'm
moving to the underground."

"Mom healed."

"But it can't happen again. Dad and I agreed that he's not going to ease up until I have perfect control of this thing."

"You do know his concern is for you, and what it's done to you to hurt Mom like that? He's not mad at you and neither is she."

"You know me too well, Sash. Can't I get a moment's peace to wallow in a little self loathing?"

"If I let you have a minute, you'll take a month."

"Will not."

"Did you see we have new neighbors?" she changed the sensitive topic in a way only Sasha could manage.

"Yeah, someone finally moved into that weird church-house. They've been renovating that place for years."

"They have a daughter our age. A cute redhead, from what I heard."

"The last thing we need is a nosey neighbor getting too close."

"Maybe you should give her a shot?"

"What, like a date?" He frowned.

"It might be good for you to date someone who doesn't know any of the gossip about you."

"There's gossip about me?"

"Tons! You really don't pay attention, do you?"

"I just don't absorb that stuff. There's too much other crap going on with my gift to notice."

"I'm worried about you, Aidan. You need something real. Nothing too serious, you know?"

"Well, why don't I just run over and introduce myself to new neighbor girl? Maybe she'll be one of those that goes mute when I'm near. Or, she might just hate me on sight. Or she could be one of the clingy ones that follows me around but can't manage to last more than one date. Or—"

"Fine! I get it. Dating's hard for you. I just hate seeing you like this."

"I'll be fine, Sash." She was right. Wendy was right. He needed someone. Still, he was so hesitant to move things forward with Kayla. They'd spent more time together lately and she seemed interested, but it was a big move for him, and something was holding him back.

He stood with a stretch of his sore muscles. His legs still burned and his shoulders ached.

"You should sleep tonight." Sasha shot him a worried look.

"I'll try."

"Don't stay out all night, Aidan. Not again. At least not by yourself. Quinn and I are hanging out later. You should come."

"I might … unless I'd be crashing a date again."

"It's not like that with us. Not anymore. We're just friends."

"Keep telling yourself that and maybe one day you'll believe it." Aidan said as he made his way upstairs to his room.

"Whatever!"

The hot shower was refreshing and helped ease the lingering aches. Aidan's stomach rumbled angrily, reminding him that his sister was right, as usual. He needed to eat, but the thought of more lean protein and no carbs made him want to put his fist through a wall. Naeemah still had him on an unyielding diet and he was about to lose his freakin' mind.

He dressed quickly and made his way down the

winding steps to the grotto to sneak a snack. After rummaging through the fridge, the only thing he found that was remotely interesting was a tub of hummus, a veggie tray and Heineken. Aidan slammed the fridge in disgust and headed for the sofa.

Screw it, I'm drinking my snack. He flipped the cap off a Heineken and took a long gulp. He scanned through his playlists and landed on Newman's *Any Other Name.* The tranquil sound of the piano solo suited his current mood. After the exhausting day, he thought he wanted company, but as soon as his sister started chattering about hanging out with their friends, he felt the urge to be alone. If he was the kind of person who thrived on privacy and his own company, it wouldn't be so bad, but Aidan craved people. He was an extrovert, but there were times, like tonight, when he didn't really know how to be around people, but he didn't really want to be alone either. The grotto should have helped. But the soothing oasis Naomi created for them wasn't there anymore. The next time she was home, visiting her dad, she'd have to fix whatever he'd broken when his latest "gift" emerged.

He stared up at the ceiling, chugging his second beer, fast on the heels of the first. The soot damage was still there. He had scrubbed and scrubbed at the rough stone, but the black marks would always be there; a reminder of the intensity of his power and how easily he could lose control.

"Dude, we're going to need some more cheerful music," Quinn called from the darkness. He'd just come up from the tunnels below.

"Want to share my snack?" Aidan offered him a beer.

"Sure, but be prepared, Sasha has Graham and Chloe

raiding the kitchen in the underground. They'll be here soon with a feast. We've all decided we need to feed you real food."

"Thank God! I love you guys! Mom's been hiding all the good stuff."

"That's cruel and unusual punishment," Quinn said.

"You sure we're not interrupting anything? Sasha said it was just you two hanging out tonight."

"Your sister and I aren't together anymore," Quinn said sadly.

"But you should be."

"We suck at normal. You know that. We're better at sparring than we are at the relationship thing."

"I've never seen anyone fight like you guys. You're incredible together."

"You'd think we'd figure out how to make it work outside of training." Quinn shook his head ruefully.

"Food's here!" Graham called as he burst into the kitchen from the door to the underground. "We got steaks, yeast rolls and cheesecake!"

"My three favorite things!" Aidan and Quinn moved to sit at the bar. "Where's the butter?"

"I got you covered, man." Graham set a plate of warm rolls and creamy butter on the counter and helped himself to one.

"You better move fast. Graham hasn't stopped stuffing his face since his birthday," Quinn said.

"Save some for us!" Sasha shuffled in with a tray of steaks and Chloe followed with an enormous cheesecake.

"Let's fire up the grill." Aidan rubbed his hands together eagerly. He'd expected to spend another solitary, restless night alone, but his friends were not going to let that happen and he loved them for it. He'd be completely lost without them.

⚮⚮⚮

Aidan woke with a groan and a stretch. After a good night with his friends and a decent meal, he felt a million times better.

He stood cautiously, testing the soreness in his legs and shoulders. It was better, but still stiff.

Nothing an early morning jog won't cure. Aidan liked to run before school. It wasn't for the exercise, so much as the opportunity to clear his head.

After a quick protein shake, Aidan darted down his favorite trail and let his body take over, just focusing on breathing in and out, taking in the fresh air and letting his muscles bend and flex. The sound of his feet pounding against the hard packed earth was loud in his ears and the gulls swooping overhead were his only distraction. For once, he wasn't brooding. For once, he felt a moment's peace.

But with his next breath, Aidan's spine went rigid and he skidded to a halt in the gravel.

Who the hell is that? He balked at the unfamiliar presence he sensed up ahead. She was young, but fairly powerful. Nothing like Aidan, but it was still disturbing. If new Immortals were in the area, they were there without permission. Gregg would surely have mentioned this girl if he knew.

So much for my nice quiet morning. He was so not in the mood for a first encounter. He didn't meet Immortal girls his age very often, but when he did it usually wasn't a fun experience. It was too late to turn back now; she'd already sensed him. She was running faster, trying to put some distance between them. He felt obligated to set her at ease. And he was curious, wondering what her family was up to. The trail looped around up ahead. If he cut through the woods, he could be waiting on her when she came around the bend. She would see him ahead and know he wasn't a threat. Aidan made as much noise as he could, crashing through the dry leaves.

"Sorry, sweetheart, I'm not actually trying to stalk you!" he called out a greeting. She could easily jump to the wrong conclusion out here on the secluded trail.

Aidan caught a glimpse of her as he left the woods and stepped back onto the trail. He expected to feel her fear, but what he actually got from her surprised him. She was … irritated, but nothing from his gift or her body language said she was scared. She cast a look over her shoulder and her red hair tumbled out behind her. It gleamed in the early morning light, matching the subtle hues of the fall landscape with strands of silver, copper and gold.

This could get interesting. She's hot. She's Immortal. Great taste in music! He could hear the tinny sound of *Pavane* coming from her headphones. But she didn't see Aidan standing on the trail just ahead of her and he didn't react quickly enough. She barreled right into him with a loud smack. They tumbled to the ground in a citrus scented heap.

"Dammit! Watch where you're going!" he growled, immediately regretting his tone.

"Sorry!" Her voice shook uncertainly.

"Your knee is crushing my spine, sweetheart." He tried to put a hint of teasing into his voice, but it came out wrong again.

I seriously suck at this.

"Crap! Sorry!" She scrambled to her feet and reached to help him up.

Without a thought, Aidan placed his hand in hers. She was warm and her small hand felt so natural in his. He waited for her to pull away with the rejection that was just part of his life, but she surprised him again when she took a tiny step closer. He didn't think she even realized she'd done it. Aidan's breath caught in his throat as he met her gaze and found the weirdest shade of green blazing in her beautiful, almond shaped eyes.

Damn. He felt something stirring in his chest, and it wasn't his power. It was hope.

She looked at him expectantly. Surprised, but not afraid. A girl his age. Immortal. Beautiful. A girl he hadn't grown up with. A girl he did not see as a sister.

Where did she come from?

She looked confused and he thought he saw uncertainty in her eyes. *Say something, you idiot!*

"Didn't mean to scare you." His tone came out right this time, but he couldn't tear his eyes from hers. *Stop staring, man. You're gonna freak her out.*

"I tried to call out before I got too close, but either your hearing sucks or your music was freakishly loud."

"Probably both." She laughed nervously.

Aidan felt like one wrong move would send her scurrying away and this strange little bubble they were in would burst.

"Aidan McBrien." He offered his hand, eager for the excuse to touch her again. "I live just up the beach. New to the city, right?"

"Um, yeah." She nodded, but her eyes were glued to

his hand as it closed around hers so easily. She was tense. Uneasy, but not afraid, even when everything about this encounter should have had her on the defense.

Aidan stared at their joined hands, uncertain what to do or say next. She was a reasonably powerful girl, but she shouldn't be so at ease with a total stranger who was immeasurably stronger. She should have her back up. She should be running away. But instead, she looked up at him—way up, and they both smiled. The tension between them evaporated instantly.

She's just a girl, Aidan. You talk to girls all the time. But not girls like this. Not ones who responded to him like he was a normal guy. Not a girl who stared at his bare chest like she wanted to go exploring.

"And you are?" he felt a genuine smile cross his face and she blushed to the roots of her crazy red hair. And then it hit him, she wasn't flustered by his power or even this unexpected situation. She was nervous because she found him attractive! It was all so normal.

Well back atcha, sweetheart.

"Oh! Um, Alexis Carmichael." She flushed an even brighter shade of red and continued stuttering something he didn't catch.

"Nice to meet you. Sorry I scared you. Bad habit of mine."

"No damage done."

Aidan's mind was reeling as they walked along the path together in an easy silence. Gregg wouldn't be pleased with her parents. There would be hell to pay for going about this in all the wrong ways, but maybe they just didn't know any better? *I really hope they aren't here to start trouble.*

"What brings you to Kelleys Island, Lex?" She didn't look like an Alexis and the nickname just suited her somehow.

"Parents' new jobs. The usual."

"You know it's not generally considered very polite to show up unannounced. But I won't hold it against you, although your parents should check in with mine. My father is Greggory McBrien and my mother is Naeemah El Sadawii." He wanted her to be prepared for any issues they might have with the unplanned move, but he cringed when it came out sounding like he was bragging.

"So your parents aren't married?"

"Of course they are." *Why would she think that?*

"Oh, your mom didn't change her last name? That's seriously cool."

"Yeah ... she'd like to think so." He gave her a wary glance. Either he was missing some important detail in their exchange, or she was messing with him.

How could she not know such a normal custom? Immortal women only adopted their husband's last names as a matter of blending in. In their world, it was not recognized.

Aidan got the feeling he needed to be careful. Somehow, he wasn't on the same page with this girl.

"Will you be going to Cliffton Academy?" he rushed on to a safer subject.

"Yes, today's my first day."

"That's why you're out here running at the crack of dawn? Nerves getting to you?"

"Not really, I've done this a hundred times. I guess I'm just trying to psych myself up for it again. Sometimes it's just easier to crawl back into my nice comfortable shell and keep to myself, you know?"

"I believe I do." She had no idea how well he understood that temptation. "But at least there will be one friendly face in the crowd. I'll introduce you to my sister and our friends."

Maybe they can help me figure you out. They were nearing her house now and Aidan was reluctant to go. She seemed eager to linger as well. He was tempted to touch her again, but with his power this time. She was difficult to read, but his gift would tell him exactly what she was feeling. He was desperate to know if she really was as unaffected by him as she seemed.

"Sorry about before." He motioned back to the path behind them, absently running his fingers through his hair. *Chloe's right. I need a haircut.*

"Sorry for crushing your spine." She beamed her beautiful smile at him.

"You're little, it's okay." He grinned back like a total moron.

She tripped over the uneven cobblestones and he reached out to steady her, releasing a trickle of his power, just enough to get a read on her but not so much that she would notice.

Except she did. *Crap!*

"You want to keep that hand?" She whirled around to face him.

"Whoa! Sorry about that, I was just—" he threw his hands up and took an uncertain step back. *How the hell did she do that?* It was like she wouldn't *let* him use his gift on her.

"Aidan, I-I'm sorry. I don't know what got into me." She dropped her gaze down to her shuffling feet. Aidan resisted the urge to reach out and tilt her chin up so he could see those eyes again.

"No damage done." He winked, but he suddenly had a really bad feeling about this girl. "You're certainly different, aren't you, Lex?" He could see it plain as day, Alexis Carmichael was a breath of fresh air, but she was also trouble.

"I don't know. Is that good-different, or I-should-come-with-a-warning-label-different?" she laughed, totally at ease with him once more.

Aidan took a step closer. His heart skipped a beat at her nearness, her scent like oranges and honey.

I'm in so much trouble with this one. He felt the bad mood of the previous weeks finally lifting—along with the pressure of a mountain that had been with him so long, he didn't even notice it any more.

He leaned in, tilting her chin up to meet his gaze, his fingertips lingering along her jaw. She was so warm and inviting and she didn't pull away from him. For one insane moment, he thought about kissing her.

"I'm going to go out on a limb and say both." His hand fell to her shoulder. "See you at school." He ran his fingertips down the length of her arm, letting the tiniest trickle of his power sizzle between them. Not for any reason other than he wanted to feel it.

He turned and jogged off toward the cliffs in the distance. It took everything he had to go. Aidan couldn't help but wonder if it was all just a fluke. That he'd let his imagination run away with him, but he was also terrified that it might be exactly as it seemed.

How could she not know what she is?

～～～

Aidan was eager to get to school for the first time ever. He wanted to see her again. Sasha didn't believe him when he told her about the Immortal girl he met in the woods. In her defense, it sounded ridiculous when he said it out loud. He couldn't wait to see the feisty redhead again, if only to see if her reaction to him was any different.

"Let's stop for coffee," Aidan said.

"You never want coffee." Sasha shot him a puzzled look.

"Well, today I feel like it. Pull over."

Plus there's a cute redhead hiding out in the café we just passed. He sensed her when they were sitting at the red light at Saint Claire and West Sixth.

They all walked along the busy city block together as Sasha regaled the others with her version of Aidan's story.

Lex is nervous. He could feel a hint of her anxiety as they rounded the corner. She seemed to be worried about fitting in at Cliffton, but it was difficult to tell with her.

"Aidan!"

He almost kept walking, but he knew the quickest way to get rid of the clingy girls was to flirt with them for a second and then send them on their way. But he wasn't sure he had the patience for it this morning.

"When are you going to take me for a ride in your BMW?"

It was a Maserati, babe, and I'm still picking pieces of it out of my teeth.

"Sorry, sweetheart, I wrapped it around a tree a few weeks ago."

"Hasn't your dad bought you a new one yet?"

"I'm afraid I am grounded, and at the mercy of my sister for transportation for the foreseeable future." He wanted to finish this up and get inside, but for some reason the girl picked today to be brave.

"Well, maybe I can take you for a ride in my little Mercedes sometime?"

"Sure, maybe." He walked into the shop with his arm around her, hoping it would freak her out and bring a quick end to this. He scanned the room for Lex and saw her huddled in a corner booth. He smiled and headed for her table. He didn't even get one step.

"Aidan!"

"Hey, sweetheart." He blanked on her name as usual. *Come on girls! This is the last thing I need today.* But they expected it. The flirtation was his M.O. He flirted. They giggled and ran away. It was all just a game.

Let's get this done. He approached the counter with an arm around each girl. He laughed and nodded, going through the motions before he sent them on their way. He never even ordered anything.

"Hey, Lex." He finally made it to her table while Quinn and the others were busy chatting with their friends. He slid into the booth beside her, trying to relax but he couldn't seem to find that easy comfort he'd had with her just a few hours ago.

"You know, I really hate that name." Her brusque tone caught him by surprise.

Okay, what'd I miss?

"It suits you," he said.

"I prefer, Allie."

"Aidan? Come on! Stop flirting with everything in a skirt and let's go!"

I wonder how mad Da would be if I maimed my sister?

He watched as Allie sensed his friends. She didn't react as he would have expected. She should be terrified finding herself in the midst of five unknown Immortals, but she just acted like she had a headache.

"This screaming harpy is my big sister, Sasha," he said by way of introduction.

"You were serious?" Sasha rolled her eyes.

"Adopted sister," he amended.

"I thought he made you up to screw with me!" Sasha took the seat furthest from Allie.

Well, that was odd.

"Who're your parents? Did they check in—?"

"Sasha, don't you have coffees to order?" He glared at his sister. He didn't need her opening her big mouth and turning this into a total disaster. If he was right, and Lex didn't know what she was, Sasha didn't need to blurt it out.

"Fine, hog the new girl. You're a junior, right? I'll see you in class later? We'll talk?"

"Sure," Allie said, completely relaxed with Sasha who was an extremely intimidating Immortal on her own. The two of them together should have had her looking for a quick exit.

This just doesn't make any sense.

"She talks too much." Aidan watched his sister move to the counter with their friends. "But she's awesome. Just don't tell her I said that." His nerves were gone and he felt more at ease now that they were alone.

"The tall, dark, quiet one over there is my best friend, Quinn. He's a senior. He's been around Sasha too long, so he doesn't talk much. The short, pale, hungry looking one, ordering half the bakery, is his little brother, Graham. He is the most genuinely kind person I know. You'll love him." Aidan was babbling now, grasping for anything that was a safe topic to discuss.

"I take it at least one of them is adopted?"

"They both are." *She doesn't even know natural borns are rare!*

"So am I!"

"Interesting coincidence." Aidan's mouth suddenly went dry. She really had no idea she was Immortal. *But how could she not know?* What kind of parents would keep something like that from her?

"The cute Asian girl with Graham is our friend, Chloe," he went on. "She's the only one of us not adopted." He smiled as they watched his friends. They were the most important people in his life, but sometimes he felt like an outsider.

He watched the same emotions play across Allie's face. Envy and a desire to belong. For the first time in his entire life, that huge gulf between him and the rest of the world wasn't there. The relief was almost more than he could bear.

~∽~∽~

"Aidan!" Sasha cried as she steered him into a side corridor after first period. "I know it's crazy but that girl has no idea what she is! How could that happen?"

"It's not just me, then?"

"Are you guys sure?" Quinn asked as he joined them.

"It's either that, or she's the best actress in the world." Sasha absently chewed her bottom lip. "And there's something strange about her power too. I find her incredibly intimidating. But I don't think I should."

"She's no more powerful than you are," Aidan said. *That's weird.*

"My gut tells me she's not dangerous," Sasha continued. "But we have to tell Dad. I'm worried her parents could be here to start something."

"I agree," Quinn said. "They should know better than to just show up like this."

"I don't think we need to worry about that, guys. Let's just keep this between us for now."

"Aidan, that's a bad idea. For about a hundred different reasons." Quinn was always the voice of reason.

"Let's give it a couple of days first. Let me get her story straight and then I'll decide how to proceed. The rest of you keep your distance for a while." He hated using his authority like that, but he knew they would do as he asked.

"How could she be our age and not know? That poor girl." Sasha shook her head sadly.

"Can you imagine? Suffering through an Awakening in complete ignorance?" Quinn said.

"Jin did." Aidan reminded them.

"True, but that was centuries ago. Surely her parents would have told her by now."

"Right? Why would they keep it a secret?" Sasha wondered.

"I don't know, maybe they just wanted to protect her from it for as long as they could," Quinn said.

"I'll figure this out, guys. But in the meantime, no talking about Allie with the parents," Aidan instructed. "This could go badly for her if we make a rash decision."

"I'll give you one week, but then we're telling our parents." And that was why Quinn was his best friend. He had all the respect in the world for Aidan, but he would stand up to him when it really mattered.

"Fair enough." Aidan nodded.

※※※

"I can't find much of anything on her, man." Graham let his hand fall away from the computer screen. He didn't need search engines to find what he wanted. Since the moment of his Awakening, Graham could communicate with computers and gadgets through his gift.

"At least not in mortal records," he sighed. "I wish I could do more, but this thing is so new, I'm still figuring out how it works."

"Thanks for trying," Aidan said. "Tell me what you got?"

"Just the bare bones of basic information on her and her family. It's like someone went out of their way to keep her as far off the grid as possible. There's nothing here but an incomplete record of her adoption and some school transcripts."

"Alexis Ann Mareé Carmichael." Aidan stared at the screen. "That's a lot of names for such a small person. Adopted by Lily and Carson Carmichael when she was a few days old, but there's no birthdate or address listed. Did you find anything on the parents? I've never heard that surname before."

"Probably a fake one. I could find out more if I could access Immortal records." Graham said. "Both are scientists, and they've lived all over the world. Her school transcripts read like a travel itinerary. Other than that, there's nothing. No credit history. No major purchases—

not even the house here. It's like they pay cash for everything. It's weird. Allie doesn't even have a Facebook page."

"Born in South Africa, then at eight months old they moved to Nigeria. Then to Egypt and The Sudan." Aidan scanned through her transcripts. "She started school in rural Scotland, then spent several years bouncing around Eastern Europe. Nearly a year in Amsterdam, before a sudden random move to the Philippines, then across the globe to Brazil, and back to Egypt. Six months in Indonesia and then to New Zealand for nearly two years, then a sudden move to Sydney Australia just a few months ago and now ... Cleveland?"

"I don't know what these people are running from, but clearly something has them spooked," Graham said. "No one races around the globe like that unless they have something to hide."

"Can you imagine? Changing schools so many times? She must be so lonely," Aidan muttered absently. Allie spent her whole life, cut off from their world, with only her parents as company. Parents who kept her true nature from her.

"Aidan, are you sure about this? Not telling Gregg?" Graham asked. "This could be dangerous."

"I don't know, man, but I have a very strong feeling that we need to be careful. I'm afraid Dad would just swoop in and take over. I want all the facts first before I tell him."

"Alright, you know I trust you," Graham said. "I like her. Probably more than I should so soon."

Aidan shot him a less than amused look.

"Relax, not like that!" He rolled his eyes. "She feels like family to me, and we protect family. We'll give it a few more days, but then we've got to figure out a better plan."

SEVENTEEN

AIDAN:

Aidan watched Allie from the cover of the darkly tinted windows of Sasha's hybrid. He waited impatiently for the queue of cars lining up at the docks to move forward. She hadn't sensed them yet and he was anxious to see her reaction when she did.

Allie was with a mortal woman, probably a neighbor giving her a ride. He watched as she made her way onto the ferryboat and up to the top deck where she leaned over the railing, her dark sunglasses glinting in the light, her spectacular hair shimmering like fire. She wore a bored expression as she gazed at the city across the bay, absently sipping her coffee. Just as they passed slowly beneath her feet, Aidan noticed a tremor of tension ripple through Allie's body. Her head turned sharply in their direction. She knew they were close, but she didn't seem to understand how she knew.

What in the hell am I supposed to do with this girl? He

knew what his father would expect him to do, but he wasn't sure he could bring himself to do it. The right thing seemed so wrong, so cruel. The right thing, in Gregg's estimation, would be to step in and force the parents to tell her what she was. If that went badly, he would likely remove her from her home and place her somewhere far away from those who had done this to her.

Without a word to his friends, Aidan stepped out of the car and headed across the lower deck to the stairs.

Time to get to the bottom of this. I'm making all kinds of crazy assumptions. He took the stairs two at a time but paused on the top step to watch her. She seemed so calm and self-assured as she stood there, like there wasn't a car full of strange Immortals just below her. She was way more relaxed with them than she should be. There were so many warning bells going off in his head, but Aidan was like a moth to a flame; he just couldn't stay away. Looking at her now, he knew there was no way he could tell Gregg. Not yet. Not until he knew her whole story. He needed to have enough of a reason to convince his father to let her and her family stay.

"Morning, Lex!" He cringed when his attempt at a cheerful tone came out sounding fake and flat. He sidled up beside her, eager to experience the comfort and acceptance he felt when with her.

"Knock it off with the Lex crap!"

"Not a morning person?" *Man, she has a really cute scowl!*

"Sorry, I guess I'm not really the bright-eyed sort." Her smile was breathtaking. He had trouble thinking straight when she looked at him like that.

"Dude ... is that a violin strapped to your back?"

"Yeah. That supposed to be funny?"

"Band geek? Doesn't really fit the whole tattooed-muscled-pretty-jock-boy thing you've got going on."

"Pretty?" *Did she really just make fun of me? To my face?* He wasn't sure what to make of the insult. "I do not play in the marching band, sweetheart. I'm first violinist and concertmaster with the Cliffton Orchestra." It took Aidan a moment to realize she was just teasing him. He was used to it from the others. He'd known them all his life, but he'd never experienced anything resembling playful banter with a near stranger before. And definitely not with an Immortal.

"Eh, play me some Bach and this cranky redhead will shut up."

She has such good taste in music! Aidan you're a dead man. You cannot fall for this girl! But he was pretty sure that already happened back in the woods a few days ago.

"You're all sorts of trouble, aren't you?" he said dryly.

"Me? You might as well be holding a sign that says 'WARNING: dark and dangerous. Keep out.'"

Oh, you have no idea how right you are, babe.

"Are you normally this mean or is it just me?" He was enjoying the hell out of the way she teased him.

"Sorry, it's me. I haven't slept in like a year, so I'm crabby. But I'm afraid the sarcasm comes with the package. You hang out with me long enough you're bound to get burned."

That can't be right. She shouldn't still be struggling with insomnia. *Unless ... no way. That's ridiculous! She can't be that young.*

"Allie, how old are you?" He *had* to be wrong. It wasn't possible, it would mean...

"I skipped second grade so I won't be sixteen for another month."

Aidan's mind reeled with all the possibilities that simple statement meant.

"That explains it," he said softly. So softly that even Chloe couldn't have heard him.

"Explains what?"

How the hell did she do that? No one hears like that at fifteen! But there were things Aidan had been capable of long before his Awakening. He could see it now—Allie reminded him so much of himself at that age.

"I'm just trying to figure you out." *How could she not be manifested yet? If it's true, she's going to be powerful. She could be my ... equal.*

"I promise I'm not all that complicated."

"I beg to differ." He had to be wrong.

"Enough about me. What's with them?" Allie rolled her eyes at Sasha and the others. Quinn and Graham were pretending like they hadn't been caught staring. Sasha waved and said something about needing to get to a basketball meeting before homeroom, but he really saw it when Chloe took a bashful step behind Quinn.

It's true. Allie was crazy powerful—or would be very soon. His friends were treating her with respect and deference. The same way they'd always done with him, even when they were kids. It drove him completely insane. Most of the time they didn't show it, but they were now. And not to him.

"They find you bizarrely intimidating."

"Most people do, but could you make the staring stop?"

"I'll talk to them."

"It's kinda strange how all your friends are adopted." She was changing the subject because she was uncomfortable. He wondered if she even realized she was doing it.

"You know anything about your birth parents?"

"Not a thing."

"Same here." Aidan listened to her talk about her family—a family she obviously loved, but he wondered how they could do this to her.

What are they waiting for? Was it like Quinn said, they just wanted to spare her for as long as they could? Did they have any idea how powerful their daughter was going to be? He could sense it now that he knew she wasn't manifested yet. Allie was close, but they had a few weeks to figure out what to do with her. *How am I ever going to explain this to her? She'll think I'm a freaking lunatic! Unless I wait to tell her after her Awakening. No, that's cruel, I can't do that.* Aidan's thoughts were a jumble of confusion as Allie rambled on about her family.

"So, who was that with you back at the dock?" Aidan asked, simply to have something to say.

"My mom."

"What? How?" *That woman was mortal?* Then it all slid into place. Allie was fifteen, on the cusp of sixteen. She'd spent her life racing around the world with her *mortal* parents. It explained everything. *But she should know how different she is from everyone around her.* If she really was as powerful as Aidan suspected she might be, then she'd led a very lonely life, completely isolated from her kind. *It's so sad! At least I've had my family.* Allie's circumstances suddenly put his own into a much different perspective. He had spent much of the last few months wallowing in self-pity when he had so much to be grateful for.

"What do you mean how?" Allie laughed. "The usual way. Mom without a baby, baby without a mom. Sign some papers, instant family."

"Right. I-ah … she's an archeologist, huh?" He grasped desperately for some thread of the conversation he was only half listening to.

How to handle Ms. Alexis Carmichael? I can't just spring it on her. It would be too much of a shock. It could send her into an early Awakening, and he refused to let that happen. She had a hard road ahead of her, she shouldn't have to deal with that too.

You could let Dad send her somewhere safe where someone could make sure that wouldn't happen. But Aidan didn't think she was the type to sit back and let that happen. She loved her family, but they had no idea what she was. He felt like it fell to him to handle this. Allie was more comfortable with him than anyone … ever, and the overwhelming relief he felt just being near her was like an enormous weight had lifted from his shoulders. They would be good for each other. He just needed to convince the Governor that what was best for Allie, was for her to stay right where she was.

ᴊᴄᴊᴄᴊᴄ

"So how'd it go?" Sasha asked when he returned to the car.

"Sure you guys are ready for this?"

"What?" Quinn frowned at the expression on Aidan's face.

"Her parents are mortal."

"Mortal?" Graham choked on a protein bar.

"And Allie's only fifteen."

Dead silence fell as Sasha pulled off the ferryboat at the Edgewater docks.

"But she feels so powerful already," Chloe whispered in her small voice.

"Think about it guys. Think about how I felt to you before my Awakening."

"Aidan! She's your equal!"

"It's only a possibility right now, Sash." He wouldn't know for sure until Allie was manifested, but it seemed likely.

"Alright, so how are we handling this?" Quinn asked.

"If we tell Gregg now, he might try to take her away from her mortal family. The only family she's ever known. And if she's as powerful as I think she will be, I don't want to do that to her. She'll have enough to deal with without losing her family too. I don't see any harm in keeping this under wraps for a while. Let me get to know her better and I'll figure this out. I'll find out when her birthday is as soon as I have the opportunity, but I think we have a little time. My gut instinct is to keep this from her until after her Awakening."

"Aidan! That's cruel!" Sasha cried. "You can't expect her to go through something so terrifying completely blind! She'll have a tremendously powerful Awakening if she's even remotely as strong as you. Don't make it worse on her than it already is!"

"Okay, and if I somehow find the words to tell her what she is, without any proof, would she even believe me? And if by some miracle she did, the shock could send her into an early Awakening. And we all know how that could affect her for the rest of her life."

"He's right, Sash," Quinn said. "Keeping it from her might be the kindest thing we could do. At least after she's manifested, she'll have proof that she is what we say she is. She won't just have to take our word for it. And she'll have the strength to handle such a revelation then. We tell her now—when she's this close, she could fall apart."

"There's just no good way to deal with this, is there?" Sasha said. "Let's just agree to keep silent for Allie's sake. I've only known her a few days, but I don't want to see her go either. She belongs with us, but we can't let this go on too long, Aidan. We need to decide this together and we'll tell Dad together." Sasha pulled into the school parking lot just as the ferry shuttle arrived.

They all watched as Allie climbed from the van and headed through the gates.

"Don't be weird around her, guys," Aidan said. "She's going to need friends. My guess is she's never had any. She'll need you guys to be there for her through this mess."

"She'll need you too, Aidan," Chloe said softly. "More than she'll need the rest of us."

EIGHTEEN

AIDAN: SIX WEEKS LATER

"You're disgusting!" Sasha shrieked as Aidan rummaged through the fridge. He was absolutely ravenous after a hard afternoon of football practice. He still had to meet Jin in a few hours for their evening session, but he needed to eat *now*. These long days were his hungriest. He would be exhausted tonight and in desperate need of sleep, but he was resting so much better lately.

"Dude, you do stink." Allie wrinkled her nose at him.

"Football practice got messy." He stuffed half a club sandwich into his mouth. She would know about the gnawing hunger soon enough. If she really was his equal, she would understand what his life was like in a way no one else ever could. That thought kept him going these days.

"I might have tackled Vince a few times just for fun." He was thoroughly convinced she would get over her little crush when she finally knew.

"Aidan!"

"The guy's a douche." *Especially for the crap he pulled with Kayla.* Granted, Aidan was pretty sure Vince had no idea about Kayla's pregnancy, but he was still a total jackass for taking advantage of her feelings for him.

He knew it wasn't his place to tell Allie the guy wasn't good enough for her, but he couldn't stand the thought of her choosing someone with such a bad track record.

"Want to stay for dinner? You can meet our parents." He cast a glance at Sasha. She was pissed at him for telling their father about Allie. She would be in trouble too, but Aidan would be in it deep before the night was over.

"Sure," Allie said.

"Shouldn't you be discussing that with me?" Sasha hissed in tones Allie shouldn't be able to hear. Except she did, and had no idea what she was hearing. She was doing that a lot lately. It was fascinating, seeing what she was capable of already.

"Uh, I can just go home, Sash."

"Crap!" Sasha blanched. "I just meant ... I ... er, how does she *do* that?" She glowered so fiercely, Aidan couldn't quite stifle his laughter.

She's so my equal. Allie's friendship meant the world to him and he couldn't wait until there were no more secrets between them. She had changed his outlook on everything, almost overnight.

"Sometimes I feel like I'm just not surfing the same channels as you guys," Allie sighed.

"Hey, it's my turn to cook this week." Aidan shrugged out of his muddy shirt. "Want to help? You can just watch, uhh ... I'll do the actual cooking." The girl was an astonishing disaster in their Culinary Arts class. It was actually kind of frightening to witness what she could do to food.

He caught her staring at his chest when he ducked into the laundry room for a clean tshirt.

Too bad she only looks at me like that when she thinks I'm not watching. But her curiosity turned to confusion. That's when he glanced down and saw Erin's latest work. On her last visit, his cousin had removed a portion of the symbols that wrapped from his chest and over his shoulder to his back. *Shit! She noticed.*

"See something you like, sweetheart?" He grabbed her around the waist to distract her. With Allie, any kind of flirtation sent her reeling in the opposite direction. She was attracted to him, but she resisted it. His power set her on edge, but once she understood, all that would change. After her Awakening she would need someone who understood.

"Yeah, the tattoos." She shoved him playfully, but it almost sent him stumbling to the floor.

She's so strong already! She was progressing so fast, he worried sometimes that she might be progressing too fast. That's why he'd finally told Gregg. He needed help getting her through these last few weeks.

"They look different than I remember," Allie said.

"Work in progress. I'll show you the plan sometime. I was thinking you might draw my next one." He quickly pulled a gray and blue Cliffton tshirt over his head. He needed to be more careful. If she started asking too many questions too soon, he might not be able to avoid telling her before she was ready.

I can't wait till this is all behind us and we can finally move on.

Allie sat at the bar and watched as he set about prepping for dinner.

"That's a lot of food for five people." She eyed the trays of meat that could easily feed a family of four for a week.

Or my family for one night. Crap! I didn't think this through.

"Er … when it's my week to cook, I like to do it all at once. How do you like your steak?"

"Just short of mooing."

"That's my girl!" He was grateful she bought his lie, but Aidan hated keeping her in the dark.

Allie's startled gasp caught him by surprise. Her heart was racing like she thought she was in danger. He whirled around to see what had her so scared. It was just his mother.

How has she held onto her sanity on her own all this time? She really had no idea how incredible she was.

"Relax, it's just my mom." He winked, trying to set her at ease. He shouldn't have said anything. Especially when her eyes widened at his comment. She was curious now. But he flashed his cockiest grin and went about finishing the kabobs.

"Dinner smells wonderful, son, but I see a lot of meat and very few vegetables," his mother said as she and Sasha joined them. Sasha cast him an anxious look. She'd just caught Naeemah up to speed and he knew their mother wasn't pleased with them any more than Gregg was.

"Hey, the kabobs have fruit, peppers *and* onions!"

Aidan defended his meal, but he was fairly certain Naeemah would insist on stuffing him with salad. She was so pleased with his performance of late, she was more and more on the clean diet kick, but he was digging his heels in. Aidan draped his arm around his mother's shoulders and braced himself for her wince. He knew she couldn't help it, but sometimes it still hurt.

"Just like your father." She hid it like a pro but he knew it killed her. That was one of his biggest motivations for hiding behind his carefully constructed facade—so Naeemah wouldn't worry about him. He wasn't sure it helped.

Aidan suddenly felt Allie's hand slip around his. He glanced down at their joined hands as she squeezed his gently. The warmth of her touch and the sincerity that came with it nearly took his breath. It struck him in that moment that it didn't matter anymore. It didn't matter that even his mother couldn't stand his touch. Allie couldn't possibly know how much that little gesture meant to him. He would move heaven and earth to get her through the next few weeks and the months after her Awakening.

"Allie, I'm delighted to finally meet you!" He barely heard his mother chattering away with the girls. "Please call me Naeemah."

"Th-thank you." Allie stared at Aidan uncertainly. She felt his mother's age and her power, and it left her unsettled.

God, I would give anything to just have this done!

"Aidan Loukas McBrien! Front and center! Right bloody now!" his father called from the steps above.

Here we go.

"Coming Da!" He winced. "I know I'm in trouble when the Scots comes out."

"What'd you do this time?" Allie giggled.

"I brought an unruly redhead home for dinner." He rushed up the steps to face his father's ire.

He met him half way and Greggory McBrien was in full fury.

"Just listen Da—"

"What do you mean by telling me that you've kept a bloody unknown a secret for over a bloody month and you want to bring her over for dinner? In a bloody text message?"

"Da I—"

"Do you have any idea what could have happened? Her family could have ties to the Coalition!"

"I know Da, but—"

"She'll have to be dealt with, son. If her parents have breeched our region without permission, they can only be—"

"Da! Will you just listen to me for one second?" Aidan pleaded. He could not face it if Governor McBrien did the right thing and sent Allie away. True, taking her from her parents and letting her assimilate safely, somewhere far away was a solid, rational solution. He refused to let that happen because he knew it would never work for Allie.

"I know you've got some kind of crush on the girl. She's your age, she's—"

"Her parents are mortal, Da!"

"What?"

"She doesn't even know what she is!" Aidan begged his father to understand.

"It's not possible. One of ours would have taken her

when she was a child."

"They've moved around so much, it never happened. She loves her parents. They're the only constant in her life. Can you imagine? Not knowing? Don't take her away from her family. Don't take her away from me, please. I think she might be my equal."

"Your equal?" His tone fell flat from shock.

"She isn't manifested yet. But she's so powerful we couldn't tell at first. It took me several days of digging into her story for me to connect all the dots. By then, we were all determined to keep her here. She senses us strongly already. She's close, Da. Just a few more weeks."

"Your equal?"

"I know it's hard to believe, but she's so different with me. So normal."

"Son, we cannot leave a girl on the cusp of her Awakening with mortal parents. It's too dangerous. Why have you waited so long to tell me?"

"I was afraid you'd do something rash. And I've decided not to tell her until after."

"After? After her Awakening?"

"It's soon, Da. I think it would be too much of a shock now. I don't think she could contain it. Everything in me tells me that this is the best solution for her."

"Aye, we cannot tell her now. You should have come to me sooner. I would have listened."

"I wasn't so sure about that," he said dryly. "She's a very stubborn girl. I think it would do more harm than good if you ripped her from her family. Just ... don't decide tonight. Let's go have dinner. Meet her. See how she is with me. Talk to her and then you tell me if you have the heart to send her away?"

"Your equal?" Gregg shook his head in disbelief. "I won't promise you anything, son. We have to do what's best for her in the long run. But I will give you tonight and I will listen to your side of it. If she really is as powerful as you are, she'll need our protection."

"Thanks, Da." Aidan breathed a sigh of relief as they made their way back down to the grotto. They paused at the entrance, watching Allie with his mom and sister as they made a salad together. Aidan saw his father's shoulders stiffen. There was something in his eyes he hadn't expected. He was almost certain his father would look at this situation with a hard heart—doing what he thought he must, no matter what. That was why Aidan kept Allie a secret as long as he dared. He was counting on her to melt that firm resolve, but he hadn't anticipated that she could do it so quickly. Gregg followed her every movement, his eyes glued to her in fascination.

"She's beautiful. And strong," he finally said. "That hair. It is very rare. She has the Indriell line in her somewhere, just like Sasha, but it's stronger in this girl. The silver, gold and copper hair was a characteristic of Indriell nobility."

"Can you give her a chance, Da?"

"Aye. Maybe we can get her through her Awakening at least."

"We could help her. We could give her everything she needs and let her stay with her family."

"It's not likely to work, son. But we will discuss it. Your mother's already sold on her, so you'll have one more on your side."

"Mom, really? How can you tell?"

"She's my Complement. We don't always need words,

although I'm sure she'll have plenty for me later. Come, let's join them."

"Sorry, Nae," Gregg said as they joined the others. The color drained from Allie's face when he turned his attention on her. She glanced at Aidan, her eyes full of confusion, but he just gave her shoulder a sympathetic squeeze. He couldn't face it if Gregg sent her away. He let his hand linger long enough for Gregg to see that his touch didn't bother her.

"Allie! Greggory McBrien, it's nice to finally meet you."

"Oh no. There's two of you!" Allie could see their bond but she didn't understand it yet.

That's it, babe. Show him how powerful you are. He won't want someone else raising you.

"I'm starving, let's eat!" Aidan brought two plates to the table. He would have to let Allie do all the convincing for now. He was almost trembling he was so hungry. It took everything he had not to devour his food without chewing. He was good at hiding his appetite, but if he waited much longer, he would lose that control.

Naeemah arched her brow at him as he slathered butter on an overly browned dinner roll.

Yeah. Ma. Butter! He shoved the bread into his mouth.

"How did you come to be with your adoptive family?" she asked to distract Allie from the way Aidan shoveled food in his mouth. He winced at the swift kick under the table. Gregg's warning to rein it in. With a deep breath, Aidan focused on taking it one bite at a time and let the others handle the conversation.

After dinner, Allie was distracted. He knew she must be feeling uncertain about his parents. She sensed them very strongly, especially Gregg. She also knew that Aidan realized what she was feeling and that had all sorts of questions reeling in that bright mind of hers. He needed to get her to relax. She was much too anxious.

"Is she alright?" Sasha whispered when Allie slipped into the bathroom.

"She'll be fine."

"Greggory McBrien, we will do no such thing to that poor child!" They both heard their mother's voice drifting up from the downstairs study.

"I don't want to, but we cannot leave her with mortal parents," Gregg sighed.

"And why not? They live just down the beach. We could keep a sharp eye on her at all times. If we ever felt like we needed to step in, we could."

"Crap, Aidan! Can she hear?" Sasha jumped from her seat at the foot of his bed. "That vent in the bathroom links right up with the study!"

"We have to get her out of there!" Aidan rushed to the door.

"Allie!" Sasha rapped loudly on the door of the hall bathroom. "We're going out for coffee!"

"Come on, Lex!" Aidan shouted, desperately trying to drown out his parent's conversation below.

She caught his gaze when she stepped into the hall. He could feel the tension coiled inside her like a spring about to burst.

I'm never going to survive these next few weeks! He could hardly stand the confusion in those crazy green eyes. She had no idea what life was about to throw at her, but Aidan was determined to be there for her through it all. She'd literally turned his world upside down, but he was all the better for it. Whatever she needed to get through this, he would give it to her. And after, when the storm settled, they would be there for each other.

EPILOGUE

GREGG: EIGHT MONTHS LATER

"Are you sure, Nae?" Gregg leaned back in his leather chair at the museum office. It had been weeks since he'd seen his wife and hearing her voice on the phone just wasn't enough. He hated being home without her, but he wasn't sure it was safe for everyone to return yet.

"Positive. She's in Atlanta. Liam and Aide have watched her like hawks all summer. She hasn't left the city in weeks."

Naeemah had been their center of communication for the last several months since the incident with Allie and Quinn. She spent most of her time with the children, but she frequented Europe, Chicago, Atlanta and Cleveland to facilitate the bulk of their communication in person. Gregg was equally active, seeing to their Senate duties and spending the time alone to dig into Livia's past. The woman was an enigma. He didn't have enough information on her yet to understand her interest in Allie. Nor why she flew all the way to New Zealand last year to meet with Lily Carmichael. The fact that the Carmichaels moved to Sydney the following day did not escape him. It was long past time he questioned Lily and Carson. He and Naeemah had agreed in the beginning to leave them out of it for as long as it seemed wise to do so, but he suspected they knew much more than they let on. He knew now that Kassandre would have had her reasons for leaving her child with them.

"There's been no sign of Quinn since they left Chicago," he said. "Greyson and Scott swear she took him to Atlanta with her, but they haven't seen him since."

"There's too much about this woman we do not understand yet," Naeemah said. "Her place in the Coalition is unprecedented. She's in a position of power and acts of her own volition. We do not know enough about her or what she wants with Quinn to attempt a rescue yet."

"Aye. For the moment we seem to be at a stalemate. I'll meet you where we planned. We'll give it a few more weeks and then we'll decide if it's safe to come home. We will wait and watch. When next we see Livia or any of her people with Quinn, we will act."

"And in the meantime, we will take comfort knowing he is not in a Coalition prison," she said.

"Aye. See you soon, Nae. I cannot wait to have my arms around you again." He knew he didn't have to voice his fears that Quinn might very well be in a place far worse than a Coalition prison. She knew it as well as he.

"See you soon." Naeemah's voice faded as he ended the call.

"Sir! You can't see the curator without an appointment!" Gregg heard the bustle of activity outside his office.

"He will see me."

Gregg shot to his feet at the sound of the familiar voice belonging to an ancient Immortal—one he knew couldn't possibly still live.

It cannot be...

The man burst into his office and Gregg's sharp bladed katara left his hand to quiver in the doorjamb beside the intruder's head.

"Lucky for me your aim is off, my friend."

"Ash?" Gregg felt all the blood rush from his face and he dropped back into his chair, more stunned than at any other moment of his long life.

"I am now known as Navid." The dark haired man cautiously took the seat opposite Gregg's desk.

"But ... I saw it done ... my bond with Kass nearly broke me when you both died." Gregg remembered the night nearly fourteen years ago when he witnessed the brutal execution of Ashar and Kassandre. There was nothing he could have done to save them. It was madness. He and Naeemah had barely escaped the Coalition slaughter themselves. The loss of his dearest friends struck him hard.

"Much of what you saw that night was not as it seemed."

"Or do my eyes deceive me now?" Gregg embraced his power, uncertain if he could trust this man who wore his dead friend's face.

"What would I know about Kassandre that no one else on earth would know apart from yourself and her mother?" Navid asked.

"Say the words." Gregg refused to utter them himself.

"She is the seventh."

"How did you survive? Where's Kass? Why have—"

"Kass could not be here."

"I don't understand. How could I not know she still lives?"

"I cannot give you all the answers yet. You know better than anyone how her gift works."

"Aye, that's Kass code for shut the hell up. It is far too dangerous for you to be here, my friend. You must be in dire need of my help. What can I do?" For Ashar to risk exposure, it could only be about Allie. He could see Kassandre's guiding hand in all of this. He had ever since he first suspected she was their daughter. It was the one thing that kept him from asking too many questions too soon. He knew it was no coincidence that her child practically landed in his lap. It was what she wanted.

"You are holding one of our most treasured secrets," Navid said.

"And a handful she is." Gregg smiled fondly.

"She is so much like her mother." Navid laughed.

"Do not fool yourself. That girl is you wrapped up in a feisty redheaded package. She's the best of you both."

"You've connected all the dots just like Kass always said you would."

"Aye, but I'm having trouble with too many dots now. That's why you're here?"

"Yes. Lily and Carson's part in this is nearly over. They can't tell you anything you don't already suspect. You cannot question them. Just let them maintain the family life they have built for her. Allie must continue to believe we are dead. It is the safest course for you both. But you all need to come home. It is safe as long as you keep a careful watch over Allie and *all* of her friends. And remember, prophecy is deceptive in that it is often only understood after it is too late. Allie's grandmother meant this particular prophecy to be deceptive in more ways than one."

"Her grandmother, the Queen? What news of Alísun?"

"Still captive and not our priority yet."

"It's all wrapped up in Allie, isn't it?"

"She is only half of it, my friend."

If you've enjoyed Emerge: The Edge, please consider leaving an Amazon or Goodreads review. Also, visit me at Melissaacraven.com for the latest news in #Emergeseries.

Find me on

Twitter

and

Facebook

NOTE TO THE READER

Dear Reader,

Thank you so much for reading The Edge. I have always been drawn to books featuring strong women, but for the Emerge series, I wanted to create a balance of equality that is rarely seen in YA books. Allie is flawed, but she is real. She will always be a confident young woman, but no one is strong 100% of the time. Not even Aidan.

Aidan has his flaws, and he struggles with them throughout this book. I wanted to show a side of him we only got a glimpse of in book one. Allie and Aidan have changed each other in a positive way, and as they move forward, they will continue to grow and learn how to stand on their own two feet as individuals, while drawing strength from their friendship and the unique understanding they have of each other.

The Edge is a result of all my years of working on The Awakening, which in its original draft, was way too long for one book. This is the "missing" content of book one. I felt it was important for the reader to go back and get to know the "before" Allie and Aidan a little better before the series continues. I hope you've enjoyed The Edge so much that you want to go back and read The Awakening again. I guarantee you will see things differently upon a second reading.

Exciting things are coming in the Emerge series and I'm *dying* to share the next book with you. Thank you for reading and thank you so much for your enthusiasm!

Melissa A. Craven

ABOUT THE AUTHOR

Melissa A. Craven (the "A" stands for Ann in case you were wondering) was born near Atlanta, Georgia, but moved to Cleveland, Ohio at the age of seventeen. She still thinks of Cleveland as home, so it was only natural for Emerge to take place there.

Today, she's back in Atlanta—for some reason she can't seem to stay away from the ungodly heat that makes her long for things like "lake effect snow" and wind that will knock you flat.

Melissa decided a long time ago that the "life checklist" everyone else was clutching so tightly in their fists, just wasn't for her. She does everything backwards because she's weird like that.

She is an avid student of art and design, and received her Bachelor of Fine Arts from the University of West Georgia in 2009. She worked as an interior designer for several years, but she's always thought she might like to be a writer when she grows up.

In her spare time, if she has any, she enjoys shopping for derelict furniture she refinishes to exercise the interior design part of her brain.